THE BIRTH OF
OPTIMA

Volume Two:

APEX

By David Hammond

For information contact David Hammond, Boilerhead@hotmail.co.uk or follow THE BIRTH OF OPTIMA on Facebook

Word count: 44858

Chapters:

1) Great Awakening

2) The Chamber

3) Ma'am

4) Operation Deep Freeze

5) Araqia's Finest

6) Left Hand Path

7) Operation Optima

8) Farewell Thief

9) Deep Trouble

Introduction

Paul Sharpe's brush with death at Old Islington Mall, now sees him being transported to safety by an old friend of his, from the Mark Quest Estate. His mission to the Red Zone had taken a toll on his body, yet his resilience is hard to shatter.

Follow (private) Paul Sharpe, as he gets ever so closer to the bitter truth.

Get ready to be entertained by what lurks ahead, in this action-packed sequel... APEX.

Let us get that little bit closer to revealing what's behind the dome... follow us as we go beyond the boundaries. Let's boot down those darn doors which have been designed to in prison us... Let's go forth into the unknown for Zuntra and its glorious Allies, because if we don't hang together, we will most certainly hang apart, by our necks.

Great Awakening

"Captain... Master Sharpe is awake."

I slowly open my eye lids down to the restriction of strange sticky mucus, that's covering both of my eyeballs.

"Where am I?" I quietly asked, blindly pulling the intravenous out of my wrist.

"Zenith, give the man some room. Here take the controls." Said a rather familiar voice.

"Where the fud am I, and who the fud is Master Sharpe?"

"Just relax Sharpe. Right, Zenith hurry up and take the controls."

"Hang on a minute, who on this Flat Earth calls their offspring, Zenith?" I inquired whilst slowly gaining my bearings, both coughing and spluttering.

I try to scan my location yet fail to do so, down to feeling extremely hazy. Various illuminated control switches and glowing screens blur my vision.

"Sharpe, I'm going to administer an inoculation to help bring your senses back," said the overly familiar voice. "It's totally benign... you'll not feel a thing."

"Get the fud away from me!" I exclaimed, as I try to free myself from the thick heavy straps that appear to be pinning me down onto a firm seat, that's completely hugging my body.

"Okay-okay, no pressure-no pressure. I just thought I'd help you out. You'll come around soon enough, and those straps will release once we have landed."

"Landed? I'm confused... where the hell am I?"

"Zenith, continue towards the opening and land her in cargo bay, seven or eight!"

A large noise erupts from underneath me, vibrating my entire body. The violent shudder forces me to cling onto the seat for dear life. Suddenly an enormous jolt occurs, followed by a large release of gas, that sounds like it's being ejected outwardly from the underside of the strange craft.

"Captain Noolan, we have landed successfully... all of the ship's vitals are in shipshape condition... well, apart from thruster five."

"Darn it... Zenith, continue with diagnostics. I need you to locate the problem with the craft immediately."

"Affirmative, Captain."

"Jason, Jason Noolan... is that you?" I stammered wiping-off the luminous green goo around my eyes, with the backs of my hands.

"Yes Sharpe, it's me... now please promise me that you'll not kick-off," said Jason, whose double appearance now settles back to normal. "Zenith and I brought you on board almost eight hours ago. Here, use this wipe for your eyes."

I begin to clean my face with the fragrance wipe and finally blow my blocked-up nose into it, popping my ears in the process.

"I'm just checking your vitals. Sharpe, what's your service number and please tell me about your military history?"

"Why?" I asked perplexed.

"I need to check you out for any memory loss?"

"Private Sharpe, service number... four eight, two five. I joined the military as a courier, as you already know."

Jason laughs.

"What's so funny?"

"Sorry, I remember them not letting you progress, down to your kush habit?"

"I've cleaned myself up since then. Once I got the kush out of my system, I decided to join the Pitster Division. I was later moved to the Alpha-Fifteen Outpost, and from there I teamed-up with the (Howling Wolves) resistance unit."

"Great stuff... well, that clears that up then. I remember you doing couriering on your bicycle, many moons ago. I was shocked when I heard that they had given you a drug test."

"You should know how strict the military are with drugs/alcohol, etc."

"Don't I just. Hey, no need for sarcasm." Replied Jason.

"I was cycling over thirty kilometres a day for them bazturds."

Jason chuckles yet again, "I suppose that's my fault then, for you joining the military?"

I reply, "No comment."

He instantly chuckles even louder, squeezing both nostrils, "I knew that (one) was coming. Anyway, where was I?"

I study Jason's side profile while he scrolls down onto a touchscreen display monitor, which is probably some sort of dialysis machine, for the regeneration seat I'm nervously sat on.

Jason's face was red and blotchy when I had last met him a good few years ago, and his potent alcoholic breath seems to be a thing of the past. I've got to say, he looks a hell of a lot healthier, yet the loss of his beard sure has aged him.

"Damn, your beard has gone," I said examining my old neighbour of the Mark Quest Estate, while cleaning my nose. "Hang on a minute... I shouldn't be here; I should be at the Blue Zone's Braxton Hospital... this doesn't make any sense?"

"I've just checked your readings Sharpe. Everything is looking good, but we'll still need to visit the medic's station. Zenith and I rescued you from Braxton Hospital last night... look, Greenshore was attacked whilst you was in the Hospital's regeneration ward." Said Jason, shaking his head.

"Attacked?" I exclaimed, recoiling in fear.

"Sharpe, Greenshore sustained heavy bombardments from the filth, who indiscriminately used hypersonic missiles on nearly all of Zuntra's cities."

"What about our (STAR) rocket systems?" I inquisitively asked, freeing myself from the seat.

Jason rubs his nose and after a long awkward silence replies, "Quality over quantity was no match for the Zakatarian missiles. They literally rained them down on us hard, destroying nearly all of Greenshore's Northeast and West side suburban regions, two weeks ago."

A sudden pang hits my stomach, forcing me to heave. I drop to my knees from hearing the appalling news and begin to rub my forehead with the snotty wipe, down to the sweat that profusely excretes from my hairline. I'm now also experiencing pins and needles in both of my legs, prohibiting me from standing up correctly.

"Damn, my back kills," I said, painfully leaning my bodyweight onto the red reclined chair. "I'm finding it extremely hard to believe what you've just told me Jason."

"Sharpe, take it easy… you was in the regeneration pod for a whole month, back at the Hospital pal. Your shoulder has healed nicely though," said Jason helping me up and onto my feet, down to my weakened legs and sore back. "Braxton Hospital was struck yesterday evening, killing thousands… you're lucky we got you out of there alive."

"Damn, what about the Howling Wolves? Oh, and those ghastly bazturds, Psycho Bill and Frank, etc?" I asked while rotating my shoulders.

"Your resistance pals are all accounted for and safe. Just worry about yourself from now-on-in. Those Teddy Boy's and Frank are still unaccounted for, but Psycho Bill is securely locked-up."

"Okay, but I still don't understand… what about the stronghold and all the Alpha Outposts inside the Circular Park? They couldn't have just folded-up without a fight?"

"Zenith… check for any information regarding those places of interest on the zuntranet. Honestly Sharpe,

Braxton Hospital took some heavy thumping... you're extremely lucky."

"Jason, we've got to head back to Greenshore, to help them out... we can't just stand around, doing absolutely nothing?" I said, with my left arm now wrapped around his shoulder.

Jason's tall bald-headed companion begins to type on a touchscreen panel on the cockpit's dash, with his back to me.

"Many of Greenshore's safer zones were hit yesterday, along with many other places of military interest, like the Braxton/Newhaven Hospitals etc, creating enormous fires that the authorities are still trying to tackle. It's far too dangerous to head back at this moment of time pal. I've also heard that Zakatarian artillery units are hiding out within the Red Zone.

I bury my head in my hands from the dreadful news, "No! It can't be... I must be dreaming? Damn, I had a premonition of the attack back when I was serving at the Pits... it was that very same morning when we were all moved to the Alpha-Fifteen Outpost."

"Really... that's odd?"

"Jason, it was strange as fud, believe me." I replied.

"I keep on thinking the same bloody thing Sharpe. The whole situation is like a nightmare on loop."

"Was there any Kreeper activity there... you know the ones who wear those exoskeleton suits?"

"I have no idea Sharpe? There was some reports, but nothing to back-up the claims."

"So, what's the plan then... I mean, what are we doing to counterattack their missiles?"

"Zuntra has been trickling many of its civilians out of harm's way to safety," said Jason, now holding-up some of my bodyweight. "We are literally like sitting ducks in Greenshore... it's far safer here, my friend."

"Where's here?"

"We are currently inside the cargo hold of Region-Five, of the Antari Ice Wall."

"Fud… so this is the base?" I asked looking out of the distant cockpit window. "They sure kept this one quiet. I remember my pal Scott telling me about this place when I was at the Alpha Fifteen Outpost, however I thought he was talking krud."

"They sure have kept things silent Sharpe. The Southern Alliance has been capturing sections of the Ice Rim for years and years, and now occupy a total of six regions out of the twelve. This particular region is where the Spectre's held their craft, however we've taken over the joint, with the helping hands of our Allies."

"Spectres?"

"Gatekeepers, Sharpe… or Kreeps to you."

"Spectres, is that their (official) name then?"

"Yes. It's what they call themselves." Replied Jason.

"See, I've been hearing so many conflicting stories about them. Is it true that they are like, err replicated biological androids, created by the Zakatarians? Or are they Aliens, from the outside of the Antari Ice Rim?"

"They are both, I think… well, they certainly are replicants, no doubt about it, but they wasn't created by the Zakatarians. If anything, they use the Zakatarians to get what they want. Think about it Sharpe, why would the Zakatarians deck them out in real gold? As for the Alien claim, I guess they are in a way, because they lack the qualities as us organic humans."

"True… But Alex Bones begged to differ?"

"Look, that man was working with the Zakatarians, the Zuntran authorities arrested him ages ago."

"What happened to him afterwards?"

"I don't know Sharpe, and I'm not bothered either way. He was an odd one."

"So come on, spill the bloody beans then… who are the Gatekeepers and why do they exist to punish us?"

"They, from what I've learnt are the caretakers of the entire Dome, yet nobody knows who exactly created them. I mean, they're not organic like us, so that obviously suggests that they've been created by something else."

"Hmm, so they still remain a mystery?"

"You could say that, but we are learning a lot more about them as time goes on."

"I can't believe that we've made this amount of progress... They sure kept things under-wraps around here."

"Exactly Sharpe. It has been kept a tight secret for many, many years, yet some have let slip."

"So, they, the Spectres have absolutely no flying craft whatsoever?"

"No, absolutely none... hence why there is no longer any sightings of unidentified flying craft/objects," said Jason. "We've managed to disable them for our own benefit/use etc."

"This craft... did it belong to them?" I asked wide eyed.

"Captain sir... there appears to be various drone footage of the devastated areas, in and around the whole circumference of Greenshore." Said Zenith drawing Jason away from my questions.

Jason aids me to the monitor screen of the highly advanced dashboard, of the mysterious craft.

"There they are... the Alpha Outposts," I exclaimed, tugging down onto the right arm of Jason. "We must go there now to help my friends. I know that base like the back of my hand.... they'll be alive and running out of oxygen. The bunker has two levels that holds everything that they'll need to survive. It's got a Medical Station and various other..."

"Hold your bloody horses Sharpe... we need to see the Zuntran authorities before we can do anything as outlandish as that. Besides, can you not see the level of destruction inflicted on both Greenshore and you?" Said Jason freeing himself from my deadweight and tight grasp.

Jason zooms into the exact location of where the three-sandbag walls of the Alpha Outposts, had once stood, using the craft's touchscreen monitor.

"Those green helmet guys will probably be sifting through that debris as we speak. They've been working night and day."

"Mickey Mcnally, have you seen or heard from him?"

"Last time I see him pal, he was a green helmet working as a part time Paramedic. He's probably still operating as one. Who knows, he might be unearthing your friends as we speak?"

I gulp, staring at the glossy monitor. The images displayed on the screen look horrific and carry with them a sense of anger, an anger that is hard to put into words.

"No Jason... the level of destruction suggests to me that the green helmets would already have their hands-full elsewhere. We must go and save my friends."

"Master Sharpe, at top speed we could be there within thirty or so minutes, however we need to repair our fifth thruster and then be authorised by our betters," said Zenith turning to look up at me. "We also need to..."

Before I let Zenith finish his sentence I immediately recoil in fear, drawing Jason's gun from out of its holster; Losing my footing as I blindly reverse backwards from the pair, I manage to stabilise myself by catching onto the headrest of the middle red passenger seat.

"Hold it right there... don't you fudding move," I screamed, with the barrel now flush with the Kreeper's large bald head. "Jason... you-you traitorous swine... It's a fudding Gatekeeper!"

"Let me explain," said Jason in a calm like manner. "It's not what it appears to be. Zenith is one of us. You must understand, we are all fighting the same enemy here."

"Fud you!" I yelled, shaking.

"Your legs are unsteady Sharpe... now please, just pass me the pistol."

"Move away to the right Jason and show me your hands... I'm not fudding about," I screamed, as both of my legs twinge. "And you, stay seated, you-you piece of krud!"

"Zenith isn't a Spectre... he is a member of the Southern Alliance... and APEX," said Jason moving in closer to where I stand. "He's not a Gatekeeper or a Kreeper... or a piece of krud for that matter. Now pass me my pistol."

Zenith awkwardly stares at me from the captain's chair and slowly swivels it around with his feet, making his presence to be known.

"Master Sharpe, if you really wanted a gun, I would have given you your own one back," said Zenith, looking into the direction of the regeneration chair, the one I was originally sat upon. "I've repaired your PPK pistol, serial number four eight, two five and have also mended the shoulder pads of your Howling Wolves armour."

"What the fud?" I exclaimed.

Zenith continues, "Myself and Hersh Van Winkle have already been acquainted too... such an interesting man and the story of the unbroken sticks... how can I say, rather intriguing. Hersh told us absolutely everything about what happened at the mall."

Jason nods his head in accordance with Zenith's claims and says, "Look... Zenith fixes things. He has been reversed engineered by the Southern Alliance to serve our best interests. Zenith isn't a threat to you or me, or anyone else for that matter."

I study Zenith while simultaneously throwing my aim toward Jason's head. The grunt's eyes are exactly the same as the Kreepers, that both Scott and I had encountered when we was back at the Pits, yet they aren't of the same colour. Its pupils have a greenish glow, and its ears are missing the large earrings dawned by the kruds.

"Sharpe, if you fire that pistol inside this craft, we will not be able to assist you in rescuing your friends," said Jason, who has maintained his calmness throughout. "Secondly, you'll set us back… wasting time we do not have. Now lower the pistol and pass it to me, slowly."

Suddenly the coms crackle from the hidden speakers on the dash, "This is the Southern Alliance of the upper-level gate section. Welcome to (Region-Five) of the Antari Ice rim, Captain Noolan. Aurora appears to have one non-functional thruster. I'll send the engineers up to the cargo bay shortly to help Zenith scope-out the problem. Stay inside the craft until we have closed the main gates… it's pretty choppy out there and the winds are brutal."

Having now heard the welcome of the Southern Alliance's radio operator I immediately lower the gun and anxiously present its wooden handle grip to Jason.

"I can understand your rationality for grabbing my pistol," said Jason, swiftly taking it away from my grasp. "Zenith, give Sharpe here both his weapon and his trench coat. We must exercise our meeting with the authorities, before we can go and rescue Sharpe's friends."

"At once Captain," said Zenith, aiming himself towards the seat that had hugged me upon landing. "The (PPK) pistol is a truly astonishing weapon. I've managed to bring it back to its former glory, as it had a few scuffs here and there. Hersh managed to retrieve your pistol when he aided you to safety, back at the mall."

"Hersh Van Winkle... so, is he here at the Ice Rim?" I asked, from having heard Zenith talking about him.

"Yes... Zuntra and its Allies have ordered all elitist fighting personnel and civilians to withdraw to Region-Five, until we can find a way of sabotaging the Zakatarian hypersonic missiles." Said Jason.

Zenith stoops down and opens the storage compartment underneath the regeneration seat and removes a large black tray, containing what looks to be my personal belongings.

"Jason, I'm still not comfortable with it," I said with my eyes smouldering Zenith's side profile. "How on this Flat Earth did they manage to reprogram it... and why does it keep referring to me as its Master?"

"Sharpe... the Southern Alliance has been working tirelessly to reverse engineer pretty much everything that lurks beyond the Ice Wall. Take this craft for instance... the interior of the Aurora has been redesigned to allow for human control, via reverse engineering. Zenith is still on his trial run, yet he's proving himself to be extremely efficient, in regard to what we at (APEX) require."

"What the Fud is (APEX) and why does it keep addressing me as Master?"

"Here you are, Master Sharpe."

Zenith both lifts and carries my equipment and then carefully lays it on top of the craft's workstation. He then turns and focuses his attention onto a large monitor screen, down to a faint beeping sound, coming from the control panel's speaker, while I admire his clean workmanship.

"Captain sir! We have four Zaka suicide drones approaching the main entrance zone, of Region-Five. They look like Zip-Nine-hundreds. There's also a large incoming Zuntran passenger liner and it looks like the missile cruiser, which was escorting her to the Ice Wall has already parted ways, leaving her totally unguarded... sir, the civilian ship is also in their flight path.

"Fud it. Should they see the cargo bay's hatch open, or that passenger liner, they'll no doubt want to wreak havoc. Listen, I'll explain everything to you after Sharpe."

"Zenith, contact the upper-level gate controller and tell him to shut the upper cargo bay gates immediately, because myself and Sharpe here need to man those anti-aircraft turrets... also relay all relative information forward," said Jason, passing me both my holster and pit fighter trench coat. "It's bloody cold out there Sharpe, so put your trench coat on now. You can come back after for your other items... hurry, we need to go."

"What's happening?" I confusingly asked as I nervously dawn on the heavy coat, and side arm.

"Sharpe, time is crucial," said Jason hitting the exit switch. "Here, insert this ear-pod into your earhole, so we can communicate. You'll need to press on your earlobe to activate it, should you need to contact either myself or Zenith. We need to head either side of those main gates. Once you are inside the gunner room, activate your turret and aim it directly twelve o'clock... keep your eyes-peeled for those Zaka suicide drones. Whatever you do, don't shoot until I've signalled... if that gate remains open, they'll fly straight into the cargo bay, destroying everything inside."

"Understood Jason."

Trembling with fear I insert the communication ear-pod into my right ear, as the rear door of the craft struggles to open, due to the forceful gusts outside, that are entering-in from the large entrance gap of the Ice Wall.

"They need to hurry the fud up and shut those darn gates, otherwise we'll both get blown out of the wall and into the ocean," screamed Jason. "Zenith, what's taking them so fudding long?"

The rear door of the craft finally reaches the deck producing an enormous bang, which is then followed by the violent whistling swirls of ice-cold wind that immediately enters into the interior of the craft, almost taking my breath away.

"Captain sir... all of the relevant information has been delivered. The main controller has informed me that the gates are jammed, and unable to close from his end."

"Sharpe, how's your legs?"

"Still tingling a bit." I replied, wriggling my toes in my military boots.

"Zenith, you'll need to manually close those gates. Carry Sharpe over to the right-side turret and then close the gates with the manual crank. I'll cloak the craft and then make my own way over to the left side turret, via the handrail on the wall. We need to shoot down those drones... hurry!"

"Cloak the craft?"

Before I can get a reply from Jason, I'm instantly scooped-off my feet by Zenith, who literally throws me over his bulky right shoulder. He now begins to battle the strong cold gusts of wind by tensing-up his entire body and aims himself for the turret post.

I try to scan my vision across the full length of the strange craft, from its tail end and watch on as the craft cloaks itself from the rear, all the way to its cockpit, prohibiting me from observing her.

The craft has now turned into a multi-faceted transparent (grid like) structure, which is now allowing me to see straight through her to Jason, who struggles with the violent wind as he makes his own way to the left side turret, via the frozen handrail, mounted to the frozen walls.

"Master Sharpe, we have arrived at the entrance of the turret!" Exclaimed Zenith, carefully placing me down onto my feet.

His biceps almost rip through his tight-fitted short sleeves as he proceeds to open the heavy armoured entrance door to the turret, which is being forced-shut by the heavy gusts.

"This wind is extremely powerful Master Sharpe... hurry-up and squeeze yourself through the gap. Once you're seated, aim your visuals twelve o'clock... I need to close these gates immediately!"

Luckily enough I find my feet. The door slams shut behind me, as I squeeze myself through to the turret's chair. I begin to lock myself in with the thick heavy straps, by pulling down on their adjustment ties. With frozen hands I then grab the handle grips of the cannons and pull down the scopes to my eyes.

My own fragility comes into mind as I fearfully look into the scopes. Zooming in to the maximum by spinning the zoom screw like a lunatic, I can now see (four faint dots) flying side by side. Two of the outer drones then suddenly peel themselves away, instantly dropping altitude.

"Captain Sir... it appears that the manual override crank is absolutely frozen. I'll have to access the main chain from behind this steel wall."

"Zenith, do what you need to do... just hurry!" Cried Jason.

I'm instantly alerted to an enormous bang and then a loud cringe-worthy sound of screeching metal, which can be heard coming from the left side of my position. The gate's chain rattles after each enormous tug from Zenith, as he pulls the chain with all of his might.

Releasing my right hand from the gun's handle I follow-up the observations with my left hand, by slowly moving the handle upwards.

"My fudding hands are blitz," I said to myself, now breathing hot air onto the palm of my right hand. "Hmm... I wonder what they have in store for us?"

The two devilish descending drones rejoin and plummet side by side. They appear to be nose diving into the direction of the blind passenger liner, that's battling with the strong currents of the expansive Zuntran Ocean.

I pinch my earlobe, "Jason... err, Captain, it's Sharpe. Are you seeing this?"

"Affirmative Sharpe. I have all four drones now in my scopes... I'm zoomed in at approximately fifty percent. Two of the drones have descended and the other two have maintained their altitude and speed. What ones do you want to take-on?"

"Captain, I'll take-on the descending drones. I'm following them as we speak. They appear to be lining themselves up to that passenger liner."

"Hold your fire Sharpe, until I give you the countdown. They are still too far away to take any meaningful hits."

"Sure thing, Captain."

I follow the drones by making precise adjustments to the freezing cold handles. Pearls of sweat now release themselves from my hairline and trickle down my forehead, forming themselves instantly into sharp icicles.

From out of absolutely nowhere, a giant grey seagull lands on my gun's enormous barrels. It looks like it's searching for sanctuary from the harsh flurries of relentless wind. The big old bird now partially blocks my view, however my D-Twelve Pit Fighter training immediately kicks-in and automatically has me peering in-between its long orange legs, towards the incoming enemy drones.

"Sharpe, one of my targets has nosedived toward your two targets. I've got to maintain visuals on this one though, as I believe it could be heading straight for us. It has obviously spotted the opened gates. Your third target should be arriving in your scopes, in approximately, five seconds."

I wipe the Icicles from my eyebrows and reply, "Affirmative Captain. I've picked-it-up in my scopes... it has now joined the pair, although it looks like it's holding back slightly."

"Affirmative Sharpe... light them up in, five four, three two... one!"

I squeeze the yellow triggers with all my might, sending the seagull on its way, along with the slugs that explode out from the cannon's twin barrels. The belt-fed-ammunition travels through the body of the gun at a rapid rate, creating a small pile of spent shells that sizzle and smoke beside me, generating some much-needed heat for my feet.

I pause to let my vision settle and watch on as the drones swerve to miss the devilish rounds. The lower gate's turrets are also in on the action and send up clusters of rounds that pepper off in all directions.

The drones now rearrange their formation and plummet downwards towards the vessel, that continues to wrestle with the malevolent waves of the vast ocean.

Jason let's rip with random bursts of fire that soar-off into the sky. I follow suit by releasing my bolts from my gun in short intervals. Making slight adjustments to the handle grips I let loose again with a volley of shots. The twenty-round cluster strikes one of the drones to my right, sending it spiralling out of control, like a fly that has just been swatted.

"One down, and two to go!" I yelled pinching my earlobe, while laughing loudly.

"Concentrate Sharpe," replied the captain. "Don't fud about."

The gate's chain continues to grind on the hidden cogs inside the wall, causing pure punishment to my eardrums, however I block it out by focusing all my attention on the remaining two drones, who've now separated apart from each other.

With ringing ears, I blitz the one on the left with a barrage of shots and can now see its red warhead piercing through a large thick cloud, that hangs over the vessel below. The drone flies head-on into the cluster of spiteful rounds which instantly ignites its warhead, causing a loud explosion, that after a few seconds shakes my gun's handle grips, down to the rather impressive shockwave of the blast.

"Sharpe, I'm having trouble with this one... it's coming in direct at eleven o'clock. These SK-Zip Nine-hundreds are extremely difficult to deal with, on direct assault, because they zip around the rounds. Hurry the fud-up and help me out here."

"Affirmative!"

Squinting my eyes at the remaining target, that's now accelerating downwards, I spit pure fire. The rounds on the belt insert into the body of the gun like a blur.

Swivelling the turret like an absolute lunatic I hit the bazturd, creating yet another explosion, two hundred feet above the vessel. I waste absolutely no time at all, in regard to admiring the debris that's now falling into the ship's wake and join in with Jason.

"Sharpe, we only have a few minutes left before it reaches this location. Check Zenith from your vantage point."

"Affirmative." I replied, taking my head away from the scopes.

I shove my feet into the metal footrest and push myself upwards. Bending my neck, I peer outside of the armoured door's misty window. Zenith looks into my direction and continues to tackle the heavy chains by tugging away at them.

"Captain... he's almost eighty percent there. Those chain links are as big as my head. I honestly don't know how he has managed to do it?"

"Sharpe, it's still not enough! Return to your scopes. We only have a couple of minutes before it gets-in too close."

"Captain… we need to cross our rounds in an up and down motion." I said while peering through the scopes.

"It will not detonate on the Ice Wall, but it will most certainly want to enter itself into the cargo hold." Said Jason, who now crosses his rounds with mine.

The drone zips and weaves away from our blistering rounds as the turrets below us come to a grinding halt, down to the angle in which the drone is coming in at.

"Fud it!" I yelled, pulling my face away from the scopes. "I'm almost out of ammo!"

My turret's ammunition alarm cries-out loudly, as I check the ammo belt that now only has about twenty or so rounds left. I peer back into the scopes and make every round count, with single bursts of fire. Luckily enough Jason manages to strike its right wing, sending it spiralling into my direction.

"Captain, the gates are completely closed," said Zenith. "Waiting for your next order?"

"Sharpe, get your ass out of that turret now! It's heading straight for your location."

I pull my head from out of the scopes and glance at the ammo belt, and then spray the remaining rounds indiscriminately, while also pressing down on the red switch of the buckle that's attached to the thick harness.

"Sharpe… get out of there!" Cried the captain.

"The buckle is frozen; it will not release. Fud-it!" I screamed, as the out-of-control whistling drone draws nearer and nearer to my location.

"Master Sharpe. I'm on my way."

Zenith rips the armoured door clean-off its hinges and launches it, sliding it clean across the floor of the cargo bay. He then runs over to where I'm seated, and tugs at the harness straps with all of his strength, totally annihilating the buckle that instantly disintegrates into tiny fragments, right in-front of my very eyes.

Throwing me over his shoulder, yet again, he then aims for the exit, "Cover your ears, Master Sharpe!"

The whistling drone gets louder and louder on approach, forcing Zenith to throw me onto a large pallet, presumably sacks of rice and flour. He then picks up the steel door that he had manhandled beforehand and lifts it up.

Having awkwardly landed on the sacks, down to covering my ears I then roll off seeking cover from the inevitable explosion. Zenith on the other hand turns to the turret with blood now gushing out of both eyes and races over to its doorway with the heavy steel door, lifted-up like a shield.

Boom!

The turret is instantly ripped-off of its bolted mount and blasted into the steel wall opposite, producing an enormous indentation on the other side of the wall. The blast then travels outwardly towards Zenith, who heroically charges at it. Before the red core of the fireball can escape the turret's entrance, Zenith slams the steel door back into its former home, literally stopping the ferocious flames from entering into the cargo hold.

The loud noise of the crackling fire sealed inside the turret post, along with the deafening alarm bells outside forces me to push the palms of my freezing cold hands against my ears even more so, whilst I observe a dozen or so fire marshals entering in from every crevice. They immediately rush over to Zenith to dowse down the door in which he is still leaning against.

The scenes are totally hectic as Captain Noolan races over with a fire extinguisher to help the men contain the smoke. The door is now finally braced allowing Zenith to pull himself away, while the men seal the door with fire retardant foam.

"What a Fudding performance. Zenith, get Sharpe to safety now," screamed Jason, who now runs over to the rear of the Aurora, coughing. "I'm going to close the entrance door of the craft... we don't want the interior engulfed with that vile smoke!"

"Affirmative Captain!" Yelled Zenith, throwing his bloodied eyes into the direction that he had launched me into.

Using all of my upper-body strength, I pull myself up with the help of an adjacent forklift truck.

"Master Sharpe," said Zenith lifting me up like a child, with its scorched arms and grazed face. "Here, let me help you... we must exercise our meeting with the authorities, but you'll need to be checked over by the medics beforehand."

Coughing and spluttering, down to the strands of thick black smoke, I find my feet and move out with Zenith, who continues to aid my balance.

"Zenith, she's all locked-up. Sharpe, I have your personal belongings, hurry, they will be waiting for us in the chamber!" Yelled the Captain, while opening the exit door that leads out to a long hallway.

"Affirmative Captain." Said Zenith.

"That was a close shave Sharpe. For a moment there I thought you were done for. If it wasn't for those last rounds you fired, that explosion could have been much worse. You literally hit its main warhead, rendering its primary payload useless."

"Really Captain?"

"Well done, Master Sharpe."

The Chamber

"There really is no need for this," I said coughing into both hands. "I'm fine... honestly."

"Sharpe... let them run their tests, so we can get the fud out of here."

"Fine."

"Zenith, go to the authorities now and tell them that both myself and Sharpe will be there... and that I sincerely apologise for the delay. Also try and get an update on Hersh Van Winkle and our supplies."

"Apologise for what? We've just fended off four Zip-Nine-hundreds," I said perplexed. "If anyone should be apologising, it should be them... I mean, who on this Flat Earth leaves two turrets unmanned? It's fudding ridiculous, especially such an important location as this."

Jason shakes his head at me, and says, "Hold tight Zenith, don't go anywhere just yet. Sharpe, it's extremely rare for them to attack the Ice Wall, because it's theirs. Just goes to show how desperate they, the Spectres are getting, along with their butt-slave (Zakatarian) buddies."

"Why is it rare?" I asked puzzled.

"The Rim belongs to them, Sharpe. We are merely like squatters in here, as far as they're concerned, yet they'll have some job at removing us now," said Jason, punching his fist into his palm. "Hence why the bazturds abstain from hitting the Ice Rim."

"I still think they owe us an apology."

"Sharpe, the Southern Alliance is extremely stretched pal, and they're becoming awfully impatient. They are battling inside the Ice Rim and on the terrain of the Flat Earth, as we speak… you've got to give them credit where it's due."

"I guess… you're right." I said while fighting the urge to cough.

"Zenith... once you've spoken to the authorities, go straight to the cargo hold and call for assistance. We need to get (thruster five) working immediately. That fire should well and truly be out by now. Just make sure you express the importance of fixing the thruster."

"Affirmative, Captain."

Zenith makes his way out of the door with Jason, who follows right behind him.

"One more thing..." said Jason, closing the door behind himself.

"Private Sharpe, how are your legs... are you still feeling pins and needles?" Asked the male nurse.

"No... honestly, I'm feeling absolutely pain-free, buddy," I replied looking through the frosted glass window, that both Jason and Zenith are both conversing behind. "It appears that the carnage which just happened in the cargo hold, has well and truly, woke me up."

"It's probably the adrenaline rush. I'll just go and collect some pain relief tablets, just in case anything should flare-up," said the nurse rearranging his own bandage, that's wrapped around his forehead. "Everything seems to be okay with you, so you should be good to go."

"Cool."

"How about the bloodspot on your left eye, has that just developed?" asked the nurse. "If so, has it impaired your overall vision?"

"No, not at all. My vision is great. It's nothing... I was born with it."

"Oh, okay. It looks really weird though."

I giggle and reply, "Thanks. By the way... what happened to your head? I can see that you have sustained an injury?"

"Oh, that... I was extracted from New Haven Hospital two days ago. They hit us hard, causing half of the Hospital to collapse in on itself. From there we, my colleagues and I were transported here. My pals were a little bit taken back by the sheer size of this place and didn't even know we had a base this big here, however I'm very familiar with this restricted zone of Region-Five. I worked here about six months ago, although I was under strict orders not to speak about it to anyone, which was hard, as it's absolutely magnificent."

"Restricted?"

"The upper-zone, where we are now, is restricted to those of the lower-zone, meaning they can't freely access it," said the nurse, digging through a box of medication. "The lower zone has seen a considerable amount of Zuntran's and Carrickian's arrive, affected by the Zaka bombardment, over the past few weeks. It's absolutely chaotic down there... hence why I like my new duties, up here."

"What's it like down there?" I curiously asked.

"It's like a city, my friend. The inside of this Ice Wall was restricted to only Southern Alliance personnel; however, it now acts as a safe haven for all, down to the execution of those darn, hypersonic missiles."

"Is he free to go now?" Asked Jason, popping his head back into the brightly lit room.

"Certainly."

I lift and spin my body-off of the reclined bed and proceed to Jason, who keeps the door open using his boot.

"Take these twice a day... your cough should fade naturally, after a day or two." Said the nurse, passing me a brown paper bag, containing the medication.

"Thanks." I said collecting the bag.

We turn right, and head down a rather long hallway. The interior of the Ice-wall is extremely bleak and needs a total revamp, obviously brought on by the battles which had once took place. Random fire stains and dents, litter the walls throughout, indicating to me that the battle for the Rim was intense.

"Right, from now on in, you'll only refer to me as either Captain Noolan or Captain... have you got that Sharpe?" Ordered Jason, now pointing to an adjacent hallway coming up to the left of us.

"Why?" I asked, shrugging my shoulders. "Please tell me that you haven't let your position as Captain, go to your darn head?"

"What do you mean by that?"

"Err, your rank as Captain?" I replied.

"Sharpe, we need to stay professional... I know I'm an old friend and that, but it's what the authorities would prefer. We don't live in the Mark Quest Estate, anymore pal."

"Okay, okay Jason, oops I mean Captain."

"Very funny Sharpe."

"Captain, you still haven't explained to me about the meaning of, APEX?"

"APEX was created by Alex Pale and Edward Xena. You probably wouldn't know them anyway, as they are way before your time. They created the organisation before the (HERO) mission, as a means of infiltrating the Ice Rim."

"I do know them actually, well not personally. They were the heads of the Zuntran Intelligence Agency, formerly known as the (ZIA)," I said, coughing. "They worked closely with Frank Sinclair and President Theodore Hammic."

"Hmm, interesting... I take it you've watched, Zuntra and its Struggle then?"

"Great documentary," I replied. "Have you watched it?"

"No... although I've heard all about it. I'm not really interested in all the politics and (belief system) side of things. I find those topics to be extremely boring and monotonous."

"But it's (part and parcel) of our history, Captain?"

"Sharpe, I just want to explore the outside of this dome... I have absolutely zero interest in anything else." Said Jason, punching his fist into his palm.

"Captain Noolan," said a saluting gentleman who respectfully stands himself up behind his desk. "I'll need to take both of your firearms before entry... oh, and that rucksack. You can retrieve them once you're done."

I pop my medication into my rucksack and instantly notice that the gold surround mirror, that I had borrowed from the Kreeper's vehicle is missing?

"What's wrong Sharpe? Hurry up."

"Err, nothing... I'm just missing something. It's nothing."

"Here Sharpe, hand over your pistol," said Jason, removing the magazine of his pistol to check inside its shell extractor slot. "How's the family... have you managed to get them transferred yet, Stuart?"

"Nope," replied Stuart, putting both of our weapons and rucksack in a locker behind himself. "It doesn't help with my wife being half Araqian."

"Ahh, sorry to hear that pal. Look, I'll see what I can do to help speed things up."

"That would mean an awful lot to me. Much appreciated Captain. You may both proceed."

We turn left, into a rather long half-rounded hallway, that has (Zeno-Three) written on both sides of its walls, every hundred or so metres. The large writing is blue (chrome) in colour, with a black surround, and has an adjacent round symbol that holds four individual numbered circles.

"This section of the inner Ice Wall is absolutely, plastered with these decals throughout." Said Jason, now running his fingers over the smooth mirrored looking letters.

"Zeno, is the god of the Zunnha faith." I said now also running my fingers over the cold wall.

"Hmm, like I've said already, I'm not one bit interested in religion, yet some people have indeed pointed this out to me in the past... like Alan Watt etc," said the captain, pushing down on the gold handle of the door to our left. "He might be here actually. From what I know, Zeno-Three is the name of this specific dome."

"What?" I said perplexed. "You've met Alan Watt?"

"Enough of the questioning." Said Jason opening the door.

We enter into a large hall, which is almost one hundred-metres long and fifty-metres wide, with various Southern Alliance member flags draped throughout its walls, at sixty-degree angles.

"What the fud?" I said coughing into my hand.

"Zip it shut, Sharpe."

"Why?" I asked.

"Sharpe, we need to remain professional inside this hall." Said the captain, leading me to what looks to be an enormous round table, that is situated precisely in the centre of the long hall.

The chamber looks absolutely rammed packed with folk who sit conversing with each other. They now pause down to our presence and after a few awkward seconds of silence, continue talking to one another.

A pinstriped suited, heavy-set gentleman directs us both to sit in a row of seats, just outside of the large round table, which is decorated with the land masses and mountainous regions of our mysterious Flat Earth, along with its vast oceans on its tabletop. We both sit down on two red cushioned chairs at the end of the line and observe the members around the table, who appear to be spokespeople of the various Allied Nations.

"You may now proceed!" Exclaimed a gentleman who's sat positioned behind us.

I slowly turn to look over my left shoulder at the elderly suited Gentleman, who's sat behind a table which holds a large fluffy microphone.

"Everybody stand!"

"Who's he?" I whispered.

"That's Alex Pale."

"Fud." I replied.

I automatically stand-up with Jason, in-sync, along with the many others. Everyone including myself positions their arms behind their backs, in-an-at-ease stance. I'm now battling the urge to cough, so I immediately cover my mouth, just in case I may splutter.

The creaking sound of high heels can be heard instantly, followed by the heavy boots of Southern Alliance troopers coming in from my right-side peripheral vision, via a rather large doorway.

A unit of armour-cladded foot soldiers march in-sync to the loud drums and then come to an abrupt halt. They then shuffle apart from each other in a triangular formation. The distant lady now aims directly for an elaborate looking chair, which is located at the large round table, while the superior trooper at the very front peels-himself away. He now slowly follows behind her and proceeds to gentlemanly pull-out the seat from under the table.

Once she's comfortably seated, he then spins around and marches back to his troops, who continue to hold their formation. He walks straight through the troops who immediately follow behind him, towards the doors, in a now reversed triangular formation. They swiftly exit the doors to the odd cough here and there. The heavy doors are then closed and locked.

"You may sit!" Said Alex Pale, via his fluffy microphone.

Jason and I look at each other, as we sit down and then turn our attention to the round table, which is absolutely enormous. Twenty or so people sit around the table, spaced apart by various monitor screens and cameras.

The distant Lady who had just entered into the chamber adjusts her microphone and proceeds to say, "People of the disc, as you are all aware… Zakataria has struck Southern Alliance cities, with an altogether (new) type of missile system, a (V twelve-hypersonic missile) to be precise."

The lady goes on to say, "We have had to evacuate forty percent of the Zuntran population to this region of the Ice Wall. Carrick has also been busy extracting her people to its regions of the Ice Wall also. Indiano and Tarokian civilians have fled to their regions down to an overwhelming increase usage of hypersonic missile blasts. There has also been sweeping reports of tactical nukes being used as well, although we need to investigate further, before we can act."

The whole place erupts with anger. Obscenities are now getting louder and louder, down to the alarming news of the Hypersonic missiles being primed with nuclear warheads, to the point that I'm now having trouble hearing myself think.

"See, the Zakas are fudding relentless Jason... fudding bazturds! They must be stopped!" I exclaimed while Jason grips hold of my sleeve.

"Sharpe, keep the noise down and listen-in. Screaming and shouting isn't going to fix anything."

I massage both of my temples, giving myself blurred vision for a few nano seconds. My sight settles back to normal as I focus-in at the disc-shaped table and those who continue to argue around it.

Jason slides down his chair with his head in his hands. He then inserts his index fingers deep inside his earholes, protecting them from the language that is being thrown about the chamber. I on the other hand, try to wake myself up from this awful nightmare, by pinching at my skin.

"Order, order!" Yelled Alex Pale, as the place now falls reasonably quiet.

The distant lady continues, "We, the Southern Alliance are making all of the necessary adjustments to maintain a new transition for our people inside, Region-Five. Our base has got enough food and drinking water to host the large numbers of fleeing civilians, and we are also running various military training hubs to bolster our defensive requirements, in and around the Ice Rim..."

"What about the drone attack that just occurred? I heard they, the (upside downers) were gifted an opportunity, to totally obliterate Region-Five's cargo hold, that is holding some of that food and water you so casually speak about. Oh, and the vessel containing fleeing civilians, that was almost struck too, right under your very nose?"

"Order, order... you will get your turn to ask your questions," exclaimed Alex Pale, toward the disruptive man. "Please continue, Ma'am!"

"No... he is right to express his anger, it's natural, however the drones were immediately destroyed by our (APEX) personnel. As we speak, able bodied civilians are being trained to man those turrets, via rotational duties, and we've also been joined by three (sea to air) missile cruisers, along with an additional fleet of nuclear submarines to help aid the incoming civilian ships. It's very rare for Zakataria and her allies to attack the Ice Wall, hence why we haven't manned all (eight) of Region-Five's turrets. However, we've learnt by our mistakes today and will continue to move the appropriate units into place, as and when they are required."

"Can the Carrickian spokesperson now join in, Ma'am?"

"Go ahead." Replied Ma'am, who turns to her right, towards the ginger fellow who had rudely interrupted her beforehand.

"Thanks. Upon entering into this hall this afternoon, I was immediately held back down to the appalling news of a tactical nuclear strike being used on Tarokia, by members of my staff, who've also stated that Ma'am here refuses to strike back, due to (not) wanting to intensify the situation. Perhaps she isn't capable of her position?"

"Order, order!" Cried Alex Pale.

The place absolutely erupts into mayhem yet again, brought on by both the tactical nuke update and the (below the belt hit). After a few seconds of quibbling the place settles, due to Alex Pale, who hits his clenched fist down hard onto the table, that he's now furiously stood behind.

"Order, order... Ma'am, would you care to explain to the honourable gentleman, and those of us in the chamber?"

"Certainly. People of the disc... we the Southern Alliance are positioning our advanced nuclear submarines in and around Zakataria, and its allies' homelands, however we are also trying our best at creating diplomatic ties with Zakataria's former Allies, to help bolster our own military advancements..."

"How can we trust the Zakatarian's former allies?" Screamed another member of the table, on the left.

"We the Zuntrans were once upon a time affiliated with the Zakatarian empire, during our forced upon communist era, were we not? And we have battled them hard ever since. The enemy of our enemy, is our friend." Replied, Ma'am.

"We must strike back, surely?" Said the ginger fella, turning to the audience while shrugging his shoulders in total disbelief.

Ma'am continues, "Should we foolishly strike Zakataria now, it would only cause further destabilisation to our neighbouring, soon to be Allies. If nuclear weapons is the road Zakataria wants to take, then they'll only tarnish themselves in the long run. Would you suggest a nuclear frenzy between all nations?"

Some members of the table scoff, yet the majority somewhat agree with her sentiments, by clapping and cheering in agreement.

"Remember, my dear Allies, that this is what the Spectre's want. They want us to annihilate each other, because we've infiltrated their home, the (Ice Wall.) They want to draw us out so they can rip us from out of this Rim," said Ma'am. "And should we allow ourselves to be drawn into their strategy, that's exactly what will happen."

"So, we just sit back and allow for our people to be slaughtered then... Is that what you are saying?" said the ginger haired gentleman, in the green suit. "My nation has got its finger on the trigger Ma'am, and we are ready to push it."

"Jason, who's the ginger guy?" I whispered.

"That's Patrick Tate... he's a Carrickian spokesperson." Replied Jason.

"Should you or anyone else give the go-ahead, Mr Tate, you'll be in breach of article seven... an article that your own nation wrote out many years ago. We must have all member nations adhere to those signed agreements, because we cannot afford for them to be broken if we are to maintain a strong alliance. Now, I want to make myself perfectly clear… I've already spoken to Paddy McCoy, your President and he's in favour of sending in our (APEX) personnel to destroy the Hypersonic, tactical nukes, via an electromagnetic pulse, along with various explosions to their drone manufacturing plants. We are in the process of sending out one of our teams, who are sat right over there, to my left, just in front of Alex Pale. APEX will conduct their mission, code named (Operation Deep Freeze). I'm certain they will carry out their objectives to the best of their abilities.

Jason lifts himself up and eagerly watches the ginger haired man. He then turns to me giving me a wink, and then throws his eyes back towards the large round table.

"When will they head-out?" Asked, Patrick Tate.

"As soon as we, the Southern Alliance/APEX gives them their full objectives." Replied Ma'am.

"And the Spectres… what happens if they, the (APEX) personnel encounter them in Zakataria?"

"Mr Tate… The Spectres will not be a problem, because they are far too busy with the ongoing war within the Ice

Rim… they are already up-against it themselves and their numbers on land, and at sea are dwindling fast." Replied Ma'am.

"Fair enough." Replied, Patrick Tate, wiping his shiny red forehead with the cloth he retrieved from his blazer pocket.

"Can the honourable Gentleman of (Region-Seven) please stand for an update?" Asked, Alex Pale.

"Gladly sir… I do hope you are all hanging in there. Seeing that we, the Southern Alliance now controls half of the Ice Wall's twelve regions, I've been informed by our military chiefs, dotted throughout the Ice Rim that we should have all twelve regions under our full control in a matter of weeks. Our Indiano troops have also destroyed their spawning systems, tallying up to almost half of their units. The Spectres are on the ropes, badly."

A large round of applause now erupts from around the table, except for a few, who look around at each other frustrated, probably down to them still wanting all-out nuclear Armageddon.

"Finally, some good news," yelled, Alex Pale, clapping his hands. "Continue, please."

"Thanks Mr Pale. The Spectres know that if we draw our troops out of the Ice Wall now and onto the land, it'll buy them time to repair their much-needed spawning systems... we cannot afford to be complacent at such a pivotal moment of history. It's absolutely imperative that we destroy every last unit, and I mean, every last unit."

"Who's this guy?" I asked, coughing into my hand.

"He is an Indiano spokesperson, called Gary Jinta," replied Jason. "And he is the one who I've been so patiently waiting to hear from."

Jinta continues, "APEX personnel have also reached the neighbouring Dome (Zeno-Four) via our reverse engineered craft, called the Pantheon. Its four-man crew have already set-up a base, along with a communication hub, hidden just below its ice rim, inside a cave system."

I stand up and shout, "You said what?"

Jason pulls on my arm and then violently tugs on my sleeve for me to sit back down.

Everyone in the hall now turns to my location (absolutely every single one of them) and pause, along with those behind me, whose eyes burn deep into the back of my head.

After a few awkward seconds, Gary Jinta continues, "We have received large amounts of information about its geographical landmass, terrain, oceans etc, which is totally different compared to ours, however the (APEX) personnel are under strict orders not to explore any further. We are waiting for more APEX personnel to arrive at their location before we can explore it to a greater extent."

So, this is where Jason comes into it. One minute he's a down-and-out, walking talking bottle of vodka, and now he's on the verge of making history.

The whole place erupts with a deafening applause that echoes loudly throughout the wide chamber. Loud whistles throughout the chamber burst my eardrums, along with the rapid clapping of hands.

"What are the people like inside Zeno-Four?" Asked a member of the audience.

"We are still receiving large amounts of data… although, I can tell you now, that the people look identical to us humans." Replied Jinta.

"How did they get the information of its landmass if they're hidden below its Ice Rim? Also how did they receive information of the inhabitants?" Asked a random person on my left.

"They got the information of the landmass via the scanners of their remote operated submersible. The people inside that Dome use something similar to our very own zuntranet, called the internet. We've been scrolling through the data and like I said, they are identical to us. They rely heavily on things called social media and communication centres to transfer information… and we have been able to infiltrate these lines of communication."

"What is between the neighbouring Domes?" Cried out someone else, located at the back of where we are seated.

"Beneath the oceans of all twelve of the surrounding rim's regions, lays the Ice Rim's inlet and outlet valves. These enormous valves regulate our sea-levels and are already known to be what creates the currents/waves. Our four APEX personnel successfully breached one of the outlet valves, using their craft's (remote operated submersibles). They informed us that they pierced through the mysterious liquid with the probe. It's now understood that the ocean on the other side is similar to our own, however Pantheon's sister ship the Aurora, will need to run tests on the fluid more rigorously. Seeing that the probe went through with ease, they followed suit."

"I take it there is a surface in between our neighbouring domes then sir?" Asked another person, writing notes.

"Indeed, however the Pantheon isn't as well-equipped as the Aurora, in terms of Aurora's exterior scanning equipment and scientific analysing devices etc. The Pantheon's main objective was to solely set-up a communication hub with us, which it has now completed, successfully. So, at this moment of time we are still unsure as to what we are dealing with in regard to the outside surface. All we know is that there's a total of four domes, situated in a circular fashion, us being one of those four. What surrounds us, and them, is still unknown, and we wouldn't want to surmise just yet. All I can say, is all four domes are submerged under water. I hope my answers are sufficient enough."

I buck-up the courage and stand-up to ask, "Sir, what's at the centre of all (four) domes?"

"We haven't ventured that far yet, but it's definitely on our list of priorities. It's imperative we take one step at a time."

"Should the Spectres within that specific Dome locate our personnel, what would the procedure be?" Asked a lady writing notes.

"I can understand your cause for concern, yet our four personnel are highly trained for various scenarios. Their exact location would be like finding a needle in a haystack. Zeno-Four's circular rim is identical to ours and the route plan derived by me (before they embarked on their journey) has made our presence one-hundred-percent unknown to Zeno-Four's Spectres. The region in which they've set up base (underneath) would be the equivalent to this region's lower level. We chose their Region-Five down to our extraordinary knowledge of its outlay."

"You said the craft is untraceable, however you haven't stated about the crew... what is it that keeps them hidden?" Asked another person.

"Apex personnel have specialised armoured suits that do not register any heat signature. I hope that answers your question."

"Thank you for your update, Mr Jinta. Captain Noolan of the Aurora, would you please stand for the audience?" Asked, Alex Pale in a loud authoritative tone.

My heart beats like mad as I watch Jason slowly peel himself from his seat. The well-built gentleman who had directed us to our seat earlier-on proceeds to Snap-on a microphone to Jason's collar, causing a high-pitched screeching sound, as Jason adjusts it into place.

The large number of people inside the chamber now stare at Jason as he goes on to say, "Ma'am... people of the disc. It is a great honour to be given such a vital role in the exploration of Zeno-Four and I look forward to linking-up with my fellow (APEX) personnel under its Ice Rim. For many years I've relished an opportunity such as this and to a certain extent I have become fanatical, to the point that I believe it's why I was born. I'm willing to proceed forth into the unknown, for both my honourable nation... and her glorious Allies. But first, we'll need to follow up with our task at hand. My team and I will set-off today and destroy those horrendous weapons of mass destruction. I can assure you now, that Zakataria and its axis of pure evil will pay a high price for its sinister behaviour."

The place erupts again, but only this time everyone stands up, looking over to our location. I slowly stand and clap at Jason, who maintains his, at ease stance.

"People of the disc. Thank you for your dedication throughout. These gatherings have played a vital role in terms of maintaining our superiority over our sinister enemies. Everything stated within this chamber is to be strictly remained classified to only those of the upper level. Alan Watt has been briefed also. Should any information trickle out from here, then those responsible will be punished in accordance with the Southern Alliance's protocols. I plead you all a pleasant day." Said Ma'am, clearing her possessions from the table.

The Southern Alliance anthem now plays throughout the large hall, producing a bassline like no other, down to the high ceilings of the chamber.

"I'll take that microphone back. Ma'am would like to see you both before you head-off Jason." Said the heavy-set gentleman in the pinstriped suit.

"No problem, Andy." said Jason smouldering the large doors in which Ma'am is now exiting. "Come on Sharpe. Follow me."

A deep sense of apprehension engulfs my being, as I watch on at Jason who excitingly aims for the large black doors to our right, like a child visiting a sweet shop.

"Listen, I've been dragged from pillar to post... what is going on here?" I yelled shrugging my shoulders. "Why do I need to go with you through those doors, and who is this bloody, Ma'am lady?"

Everybody in the chamber now turns and bickers at my abruptness, causing my face to swell-up with embarrassment, however I ignore them and continue to express my rage by grabbing hold of Jason's wrist.

From observing my reaction and increased tone the musclebound man in the pinstriped suit lifts me clean-off my feet, in a bear hug, and walks me through the exit doors that both Ma'am and the troopers had walked into a moment ago.

"Let go of me... Jason, tell him to let go of me this instant! Who is that lady and why am I being treated like this... by this big ape of a man?"

The two heavy doors now shut, with two tall troopers flanking either side, giggling. Meathead now applies even more pressure on my already lame body, as he follows behind Jason.

"Your breath stinks! Jason... you good for nothing alcoholic piece of krud! You said you'd help me rescue my friends! My mum always said you was a wrong one... she fudding hated you!"

"Relax Sharpe... The green helmets have probably rescued them anyway. I'm doing this for your own good," said Jason flustered. "You're safe as houses now. Just relax."

We now reach another doorway at the bottom of the long hall; however, this one is far more elaborate, in the sense that it's completely covered in gold, with various engravings, exactly like the ones the two Kreepers had on their armour, back at the Circular Park.

"Jason! You're a fudding alcoholic bazturd... skum sucking, stink box! Why are you allowing this man to treat me like this?"

Jason rings on the gold buzzer that has an adjacent intercom and starts whistling to himself.

"Captain of the Aurora... have a laugh, you're an old drunk! That's all you'll ever be!"

Having exhausted all of my energy and obscenities towards both Jason and his meathead friend, I find myself slumped over the muscular forearms of the brute, awaiting my fate.

What could they want with me, and why are they behaving like this? I don't understand?

"You may enter." Said the mysterious person on the other side of the static intercom.

Ma'am

A tidal wave of fright rips straight through me, of not knowing what's behind the door, as Jason excitingly pulls down its handle with a smile from ear-to-ear.

"Ma'am... your nephew Private Sharpe is here," said Jason, while the musclebound meathead struggles with my deadweight, down to the lengthy duration of carrying me. "Andy, you can let go of him now pal."

The powerlifter carefully lowers me onto my feet as the mysterious lady draws in closer.

"What the fud are you on about?" I yelled, violently coughing into my hands, from nearly having my lungs forced-out of my throat.

I kneel down on one knee to help catch my breath, while at the same time, try my utmost best to figure-out as to what this alcoholic idiot could be going on about?

"I don't have an aunt, you twat," I said, looking up at the mysterious lady, who now comes into full view. "Mother?"

"Bless him. Andy, help him up... why was you being so rough with him?"

"Zenith told me that your nephew here had a (hissy fit) on board the Aurora. I was only being cautious Ma'am. It's imperative to follow-up on security procedures at all times."

"I'm hardly going to harm my own people... you're an absolute knucklehead!" I exclaimed, smouldering Jason who now cuts his eyes at me. "And as for you... you woke me up after a month of being in regeneration, while you're cozying up to a reprogrammed Kreeper. What was I supposed to do... give you both a hug and a kiss?"

"Look, I'm sorry. I merely told Zenith to tell Andy here, to be cautious with you," said Jason gripping my shoulder. "I'm sorry. Look, you need to remain here from now on in, under the strict orders of Ma'am… and I know you're going to kick-off, but you must listen to me Sharpe, it's for your own good."

"I'm not staying here… I have absolute zero connection with this lady whatsoever. She may very well be my aunt, but that doesn't give her full control over me."

"No… it's my own fault," said Ma'am drawing me in with a tight squeeze. "Paul, it was me who gave both the Captain and Zenith, their orders to extract you from Braxton Hospital. It didn't enter my mind for one minute, as to what your reaction to Zenith could have been like, so I truly apologise. Relatives of all higher-ranking personnel, have been cleared to assemble their families here."

"Mum never said anything about her having an identical twin sister," I remarked, with a prolonged gaze into my aunt's eyes. "Where are my siblings then?"

"Your brother (Thomas) is still serving on the Phoenix and your sister is currently working within Region-Four, as a nursery teacher. You will need to remain with me here. Andy, you can show Paul to his quarters, just down the hall."

"Yes, Ma'am."

"No, no... hang on a minute, I'm not staying here. Didn't you hear me already," I said turning to Jason. "Jason, you didn't say anything about me being confined to any quarters?"

Ma'am intervenes, "Paul, we are at war... you must remain here with me. I've already planned for you to stay here. You'll have your own cabin with a nice bed and washing facilities. I've even went to the trouble of getting you a computer games console."

"No! See, you're still not listening to me? Where was you when (we) was living in squalor with Mum, at the Mark Quest Estate? Where was you when (my Mum) your sister died? Where was you when I was serving at the Pits and Alphas? Where was you when I was almost killed in Old Islington Mall? You was nowhere to be bloody seen... so what gives you the right to tell me what to do now? Sorry, but I don't even know you?"

After an awkward moment of silence, Andy salutes Ma'am and says, "Sorry Ma'am, but I'm due to man the upper-level security desk shortly... asking for your permission to leave?"

Ma'am finally drops her head from my ambush of questions and awkwardly stumbles, "Andy, you, you may leave."

"One more thing... does that mean I can have my console back?"

"Andy... just go." Replied Ma'am.

Andy departs our circle and aims for the exit, while admiring his pumped-up physique in the reflective gold door.

"Ma'am... you can't keep Sharpe against his own will; besides he's still contracted to military duties. Should they find out that he's here, they'll most certainly draw him back into duty. No offence Ma'am, but I did highlight this to you prior to us extracting him from Braxton Hospital."

"Sorry, but I'm still confused as to why my mother never spoke about you... why is that?"

"This isn't the time and place Sharpe." Expressed Jason, crossing his arms.

"No Captain, Paul deserves to know the truth. My duties here have caused too much pain and suffering to my extended family. The only memory I have left of your mother, is her children... and it's my duty to protect you and them at all costs. I've missed her so much since the last time we were together, and will hold that night, especially in my memory for years to come. I've been turning those distant memories over and over again lately, in my mind's eye and will continue to do so. Captain, Jason Noolan, was assigned as your families very own minder when you all lived in the Mark Quest estate."

"Ma'am... please, stop."

"Continue," I said studying Jason's body language. "Please continue?"

"Jason has always known about the importance of keeping you and your siblings safe. He has always followed-up on my orders, which have only stood as a means of protecting my loved ones."

"Jason, you knew my mother had a twin sister... and you said absolutely nothing!"

"Sharpe, it's not what you perceive it to be. I'm given my orders, and I follow up with them," said Jason, gesturing with his hands for me to calm down. "Everything I've ever done was to only protect your mother (yourself) and your siblings."

"So, Islington Mall... where was you then Jason, when I almost got killed by the skum... and their buddies the Teddy Boys? Oh, and let's not forget about the krud I endured at the Pits?"

Ma'am responds, "Paul, the mission to the mall wasn't meant to have happened... it was a total blunder. We had organised with the (Screaming Hawks) to take you in for extraction, to Region-Five, because we had foreknowledge of (pending) hypersonic missile attacks. However, they informed us of a switch, that had occurred, due to General Legos and his second in command General Barric."

Shocked by what I've just heard, I instantly say, "What?"

Ma'am continues, "We was later informed by Hersh, that Frank, General Barric's nephew, was working with the Zakas, via his affiliation with the Teddy Boy's. He also told us that Frank took out that specific resistance group. Legos unknowingly made the switch down to you being more familiar with the mall. Barric has since been charged for aiding Frank and is due to be executed tomorrow morning."

"No, no way… Barric deserves a thorough investigation. Frank was working alone," I exclaimed. "You've got to tell them to stop. Barric's parents aided both Carol and Theodore Hammic, to safety back in Zakataria. You've got to inform them. He's innocent."

"Relax Sharpe," said Jason, giving Ma'am the nod. "We will sort it out immediately."

"You knew about the pending attacks?" I asked.

"No… we had some really sketchy information, that just wasn't enough to act upon." Replied Ma'am.

The memory of the nightmare/premonition I had back at the Pits still lingers in my mind and continues to plague me. Who, or what was it that was trying to warn me of the pending missiles and the exoskeleton wearing Spectres?

Ma'am picks up the handle of an old red rotary phone that's sat adjacent to her and spins its dials in a panic.

"Marcus… get in touch with command and tell them to abort all of Region-Four's executions, tomorrow… what do you mean they've been brought forward?" Yelped Ma'am on the phone, shaking.

Ma'am now rubs her left temple with her index finger and says, "Marcus, we may still have time. Barric has a witness called Private Sharpe, military number, four eight, two five… I repeat, four eight, two five. If they want to interview him, they can. He's here to testify…. no problem."

Imagine if I didn't have that conversation with Barric when I was in the entertainment room, about President Hammic? That little secret of his, about his parent's affiliation to Carol and Theodore, may very well have saved his life.

"Darn it," said Jason rubbing his nasal bone. "The C-sectors will end up handing Sharpe over to the military, straight after the interview."

I reply instantly, "So what… what's the fuss? My friends are probably struggling to breathe in that bunker, back at the Alpha Base… I must return to my military duties immediately."

Ma'am now seems choked as she goes on to say, "Sharpe the hypersonic missiles are killing far too many troopers. I fear that you may come to extreme harm. Jason, think of something fast... what other options do we have?"

Jason starts to walk around in circles like a man possessed and then abruptly turns to us to say, "We sign him up to (APEX). Call Alex Pale Immediately Ma'am and tell him to forge an application form. Tell him time is critical and that I've recommended Sharpe."

Ma'am pulls out a writing pad, shaking, "Paul, sign here. I'll take your signature to Alex Pale now and get him to add it onto your application form."

An awkward silence lingers over us.

Military or APEX... what will it be? Perhaps I can get in on the mission to Zeno-Four, should I perform well on the mission to Zakataria. Hmm, and I still have to save my friends at the Alpha Outpost.

"Okay... but Jason, you must help me save my friends at the Alpha base."

"Fine… just sign the paper."

I sign on the dotted line to the annoying sound of the rotary phone, that literally bounces around the glass table to every ring.

"Marcus… right okay. That's great news," said Ma'am resting the phone's handle on her shoulder. "C-sectors are on route to my quarters… what?"

Ma'am violently slams down the phone, and proceeds to push us out the door, and into the hallway that leads to the large chamber.

"They've stalled the executions. Go to the Cargo hold now. Don't look back. I'll take this to Alex Pale's quarters now and sort everything out at my end. Should you see the C-sectors, please avoid contact… get on board the Aurora and I'll contact you."

"Ma'am," said Jason in a saluting pose. "Please try and fast track Stuart's application… the poor fudder hasn't seen his family for months."

"I'll see what I can do… now go!"

We both head out the Chamber and turn left towards the hall in which we had entered into earlier-on, to retrieve our items.

"Honestly, should I get cleared for APEX, you must promise to help me save my pals at the Alphas?"

"Please Sharpe… we need to get the fud out of here before those C-sectors show-up," said the captain, apprehensively turning the corner. "Don't worry, I'll help you retrieve your friends. I promise."

"Ah, Stuart! My dear friend. Have you seen any C-sectors?"

"Nope… why, Captain?"

"I need you to do me a big favour," said Jason looking down the hall like a hawk. "They will be here shortly. I need you to demand they remove their weapons."

"But Captain, they're C-sectors... they are not required to do so by law?" Said Stuart with hands on hips.

"Right okay. I want you to hold them here for as long as you possibly can. I don't know... you'll have to make something up? I've spoken to Ma'am, and she has promised to move mountains to fast-track your family's application form."

"You don't know how much that means to me Captain." Said Stuart passing us our items.

We collect our pistols and slot them into our holsters, along with my rucksack that I immediately throw over my shoulder.

"Right... Here, take my swipe card and enter through that door opposite," said Stuart, looking down the long hall towards three C-sectors, who are now marching to his checkpoint. "Go... I'll toy with them. Follow the hall to the last door on the right. You'll know where you are when you exit. Leave my swipe card with one of the engineers... go now."

Jason swipes the card reader and pushes the door open to the sound of the marching boots, who are now only eight or so meters away.

"Fud... what is this place?" I asked quickly closing the door behind myself.

"This is where they hold the Spectre's craft. There's around eighty or so craft here, all awaiting to be revamped for human control. We must hurry. We cannot stay here."

We pass an enormous number of flying craft that sit majestically behind a continuous observation window. The large fleet of craft have teams of men welding various parts onto their aerodynamic exterior shells.

"The Aurora, along with these other craft look awfully similar to dragons, don't you think?"

"Hmm, I can't really say that I can see it, to be honest, Sharpe?"

"Yeah, look at the front end... it's like a dragon's head. And now look at the body, and the short wings..."

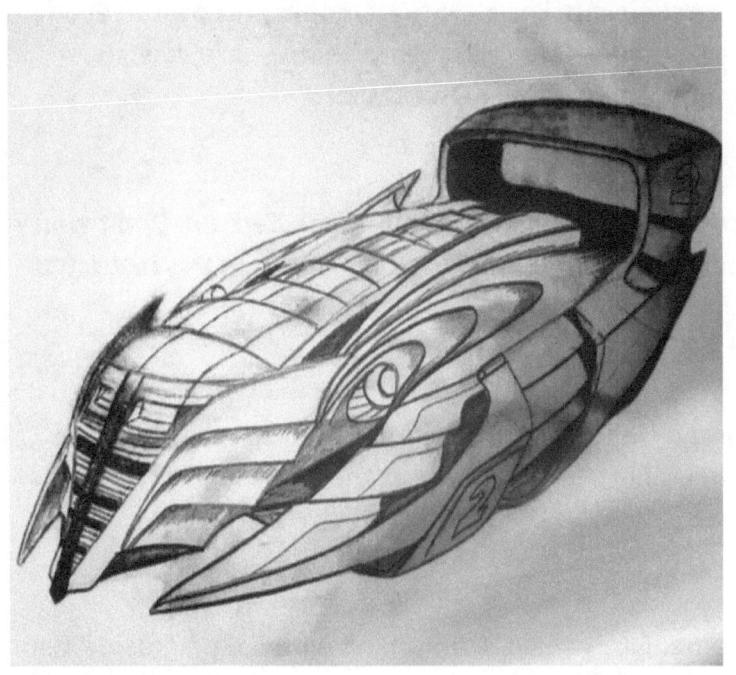

"Ahh, yeah, I can see it now," said the captain stopping to observe my findings, "The wings actually extend in flight, so yeah, I suppose they do look like dragons.

"Captain Noolan... this is a surprise." Said a rather familiar voice behind us.

We both turn around.

"Mr Watt... I'm on a mission to destroy those (V-twelve) hypersonic missiles etc. Stuart lent me his pass to evade the C-sectors. Both myself and Sharpe here, have been ordered to make haste, by Ma'am."

"You needn't explain yourself to me Captain. Don't worry about them either, they're not allowed in this restricted zone."

"Great. Hello Ron." Said the Captain, kneeling down to stroke Alan's dog, who sits at the legendary researcher's side.

I immediately shake Alan's hand with a tight grasp, "Alan, Alan Watt... it's an absolute honour to meet with you sir. I've been listening to your talks for many years. I honestly can't believe that I'm actually stood here with you. I've got so many questions that I would love to ask you?"

Alan tips his fedora and winks, "The pleasure is all mine. By the way, Captain, I heard your speech at the Chamber. You are the right man for the job, indeed. I'm heading to Ma'am's quarters now. I've been ordered to stay extremely quiet about the many breakthroughs expressed in the Chamber by Jinta and will only trickle out such information to the masses, when I'm given the heads-up."

"She will not be there. Ma'am will be with Alex pale," said The Captain, scratching behind the bulldog's ears. "Sharpe and I here must dash."

"That's understandable Captain."

"Sharpe here, is an avid listener of yours." Said the Captain now standing at ease.

"Perhaps when we aren't all in such a mad rush, we can all meet-up for a couple of jugs of fine Carrickian stout," replied Alan, "Myself and Jinta are writing out your main objectives in regard to your mission to Zeno-Four, which is solely based on our own research, from the stacks of information we've received from Pantheon's crew."

"Sounds interesting... there's absolutely no doubt in my mind that your objectives will offer us some great challenges, challenges that I'm eager to take-on." Replied the Captain.

"That would be fantastic sir. I'm going to hold you to that drink. I've just got one question though?" I asked in absolute awe from meeting one of my prized researchers.

"Go ahead son?"

"What happened to Alex Bones, the independent researcher? I've heard absolutely nothing about him... apparently, he attacked you down to your Flat Earth research?"

"Oh, him. Alex Bones wasn't independent... he was bought-out with kredits. They the Zakatarians owned him. He's now locked-up within this Region. Shills and upside downers like himself do not deserve the freedom to impose pure lies. I believe he is sharing a cell with Mr Mitre, the puppet politician primed by the Zakatarians."

"So that's what happened to him. I can't believe they are being held here? I'll admit, I was taken in by all of his lies when I was a teenager." I replied while kneeling down to stroke the wrinkled-up bulldog.

"Yes... Mr Bones was financed by the enemy. He was good at his job, mind; however, he ended up being consumed by his own lies, in the bitter end. Folk like himself will dish out half-truths, but the other half will be pure lies, used just to deceive."

"Interesting." I said with an intrigued head on.

"Take the laser beams for instance, the ones in which we had shot across large bodies of water, lakes, rivers etc, before the (Hero) mission. We was shooting them across hundred-upon-hundreds of miles, yet the beams remained perfectly level. Where there should have been curvature, there was absolutely none."

"I didn't know you had shot them at such long distances? I thought they were only, forty/fifty kilometres?"

"Ah, see that's because Alex Bones had edited my video evidence. Himself and his crooked team would then distribute our video experiments, which would then show much lesser distances. This was merely done to demonise us."

I promptly say, "Right, thanks for answering my question, sir. The reasoning behind Alex Bone's demise has always bugged me. I'm glad it's now at rest."

"The pleasure is all mine, son."

"Sharpe, we must head-off. Those C-sectors will be searching high and low for us." Said the Captain while I stroke the dog's head, who's now wagging its stumpy tail.

Alan laughs, "Ron appears to like you. Listen chaps, I best be off. May your god or your gods go with you."

"Cheerio Alan, and Ron."

Having said my farewell, we exit the last door on the right.

Jason scratches his head, and says, "Sharpe, this way. Some of these C-sector's wear face recognition cameras... we must remain cautious. If they collar you before your APEX application goes through, you'll be escorted back into the military."

"Okay... just chill." I replied.

May your god or your gods go with you... that's how Alan addressed his listeners at the end of every talk. Man, I can't believe I've actually met the main man himself. Damn, wait until Scott finds out that I met his hero.

We finally make it to the cargo bay and walk through the middle of ten or so engineers, that are loitering near to the rear of our craft.

"Captain, I said some horrible things back in the chamber. None of them are true... I'm terribly sorry. I feel utterly foolish."

"Sharpe, now's not the time," said the captain, aiming for Zenith. "We need to get you out of here before you get flung head-first back into the military. Zenith, is the (EMP) on the ship?"

"Affirmative Captain. The electromagnetic pulse is strapped into place."

"And thruster five," asked the captain. "Has it been rectified?"

"Affirmative. The module has been replaced... we are just synchronising it to the on-board computer system."

"We need to go now... how long will it take?"

"Ten minutes or so, Captain."

"Fud it… and the gates are they fully operational?"

"The gates main fuse has also been replaced, along with its cell management components and eternal locking switch. Its main power supply was down; however, I changed its pulse fuse along with its hex-module indicator…"

"Enough of your quibbling Zenith… I didn't ask you to tell me the (ins and outs) of a fudding duck's arse," yelled the captain. "Sharpe, get on board the Aurora now… and stay inside!"

"At once, Captain."

"Hold it right there! Private Paul Sharpe, service number, four eight, two five, of Alpha-Fifteen Defence Post. A code has been assigned to us for your safe escort to our interview department at the lower level. Upon further investigations carried out by us, you my friend are being recalled for military duty afterwards. You'll need to comply with our orders… so please step away from the craft and join us here."

The cargo bay falls into a deafening silence, as the large group of rowdy engineers now whisper to each other, whilst staring at my every move.

I gulp, "Captain?"

"Sharpe," quietly said the captain, shaking his head. "I'm powerless without your APEX Identification card. You'll have to conform... otherwise they'll arrest you, causing yet more hurdles for us."

I turn to the C-sectors and say, "I'm a member of (APEX) now. I'm contracted with them, so I will have to reschedule the interview with you guys, as I'm due to head-out from being briefed on important objectives."

"We checked our system ten minutes ago. It states that you are to be interviewed and are then expected to resume military service. Stop messing us about Private... show us your APEX identification card to clarify this claim?"

I turn to the perplexed Captain while exaggeratingly frisking my own pockets, in order to stall them a little. After a few awkward seconds of having no evidence, I take it on the chin and accept my fate, by saluting the captain who stands absolutely deflated.

"What about my friends at Alpha Fifteen?"

"I stand by my word, Sharpe. Me, Zenith and Hersh will head there straightaway… I promise."

"We haven't got all day!" Yelled the Jobsworth C-sector.

"Come on chaps, you'll not be needing the handcuffs… it's a little extreme, don't you think?" I said observing the eager one to my left, who appears to be extremely overzealous. "I've not committed any crime… yet?"

"Wasting our time, is a crime. You could have settled this when we was in the hall, yet you chose to swerve us. It's a criminal offence to avoid C-sectors. It almost feels as if you were trying to abscond from us… could it be down to you resuming military duties?"

"Yes… your probably right chief. Now hand over your pistol," said the one on my left. "Or I'll take it from you… by force."

"Okay." I said, slowly unclipping my holster.

I spot Stuart, the guy from the weapons checkpoint desk in my left side peripheral. He appears to be waving a glossy identification card in the hallway. Stuart enters the cargo hold and stealthy manoeuvres himself around the back of the C-sectors, without them even noticing him.

"Sharpe... you forgot this," said Stuart, red faced and out of breath. "It was left in the pistol locker."

"Hold it right there. This is C-sector business... now step aside!" Exclaimed the Jobs worth on the left.

I swiftly take the card and shout, "Fantastic! There you go... see, I'm a member of APEX."

All three C-sectors now look at each other in total shock, as the surrounding engineers in the cargo hold chuckle to themselves.

"So, chaps... it looks like you are now wasting our time," said the captain, with a smirk from ear-to-ear. "We will link up for an interview on our return... Sharpe, jump on board."

"Right-on Captain." I replied as the C-sectors argue with each other, out of the cargo hold.

"Oh, Stuart here's your swipe card. Look, I'll make sure your family is sorted out, trust me."

"Ma'am had a chat with me before she gave me Sharpe's card. She told me to tell you to make tracks immediately. Thanks ever so much for sorting it out, Captain."

"No, honestly, the pleasure is all mine, Stuart."

We both clamber onto the ship, to the sound of the cargo bay's gates that grind and creak.

"Sharpe, Stuart certainly saved your bacon."

"Tell me about it!"

"Zenith, where's Hersh," asked the captain, buckling himself into the seat to my right, "he best hurry."

Zenith turns at me with a welcoming nod and then bends his neck to observe the rear door, "Welcome aboard Master Sharpe. Hersh is here Captain."

I immediately turn and watch on as Hersh lays down the supply holdalls. He then buckles himself into a passenger seat, located at the very rear of the craft.

Hersh turns right and throws a thumb-up into the air, as the door closes. He then looks directly at me and lifts the peak of his cap, showing off his signature large malar bags under his tormented eyes.

The craft now lifts up and exits the cargo-hold at a phenomenal speed. We sore into the sky, gaining altitude rapidly and then veer to the left, causing my stomach to spasm. The speed of this craft is extraordinary, and its manoeuvrability is tight as fud.

"Captain... all systems are functional," said Zenith, checking the control screen." We should arrive at the Alpha location in precisely fifteen minutes."

"Fud me," I exclaimed. "That's quick!"

"Sharpe, I did make a promise to you that we would help save your friends... I'm a man of my word," said the captain steering the craft. "But you must promise me from now on in, that you'll adhere to my every command."

"Captain sir... yes sir. I promise."

"Great!" Replied the Captain.

Our bodies bounce around to every thick cloud we pierce through.

"Hersh, how are you? Oh, and how are the rest of the team?"

"I'm fine. The guys are all good. Josh was asking for you actually. How's your shoulder my friend?"

"It's healed up nicely. Hey, thanks for aiding me to safety back at the mall. I owe you one. Josh, Yogi and Jhita are all fine men."

"No... don't thank me. It was a team effort. Just remember the story about the sticks. One day you may need to do the very same thing?" Replied Hersh.

"Hopefully not, but I'm ready willing and able," I replied. "Captain, I've been meaning to ask you about APEX?"

"Go ahead Sharpe?"

"Where was Edward Xena, Alex Pale's right-hand man? I didn't see him in Region Five's Chamber?"

"That's because he was killed by the Spectre. They apparently had explosives concealed in their abdomens. One of them failed to detonate... and I guess the rest is history."

"What?"

"Yeah, the C-sectors brought them in for questioning. I'm not entirely sure what happened prior, but he did indeed die by the blast."

"We, Scott and I brought them in during investigation procedures, but we wasn't told anything about them killing Edward Xena."

"So, it was the D-twelve division who brought them in... it did enter my mind at the time, that it may have been you guys, however I didn't have the information." Replied the Captain.

"Yeah, it was us... damn, they could have killed us both."

"It's been kept quiet down to us not wanting to give them the satisfaction of the assassination."

"That's wild." I replied.

"Captain... initiating cloak, in approximately five seconds." Said Zenith pushing the buttons of the craft's control panel.

The southern coastline of Zuntra now falls into view from the cockpit's window. Plumes of black smoke rise from the city's industrial Blue Zone, literally blocking my view from observing the River Tear.

"Zenith, Keep the radar locked into the northwestern district and also keep me informed of any aerial threats, that may come our way."

"Captain, I've set up a landing pin on the main map. Follow that flight path and land her behind the remaining scattered sandbags."

"Got that. Coming into land in approximately twenty seconds. Hold on tight men." Said the Captain.

The craft rattles with violence as we descend and its buffering thrusters beneath us chucks up dust and debris. The rumble now begins to settle and is suddenly overpowered by the hydraulic landing gear.

"Zenith, check all thrusters."

"Captain, we are looking good. All systems are green and thruster five is working as it should."

We successfully land beside the base and simultaneously release our buckles to the sound of the engines that slowly wined themselves down to a tranquil hum.

"Zenith, switch-off the main engines and keep her cloaked, while we go out to investigate."

"Affirmative Captain."

"Sharpe, Hersh... stay close to me."

We all exit the craft one by one and then proceed to where the bunker entrance once stood.

The sandbag wall that had served as a buffer wall is now only half its size, down to the scorched bulky sandbags being blown across the base. The odd fire here and there, still rages on and offers exceptional cover for us as we move in closer for investigation.

"Captain, look at those large footprints... the Spectre were definitely here. The prints are far too big, to be that of a Zakatarian soldier." I said coughing into my hand.

"Hmm, it appears you're right."

"They was wearing the exoskeleton suits, just like the ones I encountered in my premonition, along with the ones I was fighting back at the Mall." I said wiping the sweat from my brow.

"Strange." Replied the Captain observing the indentation of the rippled tread."

"Very peculiar... there's definitely something in that premonition. It was almost like I was being warned by a higher intelligence?"

"Take off your tinfoil hat, Sharpe."

"Well, it happened to me, okay. For fud sake."

"Sharpe, where is the hatch?" Asked the Captain wiping his saturated forehead with a flannel.

"It's right here, however it looks like it's buried under all of these scattered sandbags... we need Zenith to remove them at once."

The captain presses onto his right earlobe, "Zenith, put your sunglasses on and get out here... we need your help. Make sure you wear those darn glasses... I don't want you startling anyone else. Hurry up, our time here is extremely limited."

Zenith spritely races over from the back of the Aurora, in a pair of shades that wrap around his head, prohibiting folk from seeing his green artificial Kreeper's eyes.

"Should there be any survivors, how do you suppose we get them to safety?" I asked.

"Hersh! There's a MAS truck buried underneath those burning bags. Reverse her out. Once it's free, turn off its engine and report back to me."

"Okay Captain."

Zenith goes to town on the fallen sandbags by lifting and throwing them at the side of himself.

"Captain sir. The hatch appears to be locked from inside." Said Zenith.

"See, I told you. I know the bunker's layout very well... they obviously locked themselves in," I said banging on its hatch. "Although, they would have had everything they would have needed to survive... trust me."

"Open the hatch, it's me, Sharpe!"

The hatch instantly unlocks and slowly lifts open to the sound of Legos, who drunkenly sings Zuntran war songs. He stumbles out bare-chested and swigs his whisky like an old drunken sailor, whose ship is battling a treacherous thunderstorm.

"Where are they, and what was that loud rumbling sound?" screamed the General. "I'll skin them if I get my hands on them!"

I immediately yell, "Fud me! General, why on this Flat Earth are you drinking like that?"

Various others crawl out gasping for air with injuries to their saturated sweaty bodies.

"Taylor! Scott! Louie!" I frantically screamed into the stinking hatch.

Taylor finally comes up battered and bruised and showing extreme signs of emotional torment. His autopilot trance and body language suggests to me that he's in a dark place. It's almost like I'm invisible to him?

Drowning in outright fear I instantly ask, "Taylor, where is Scott and Louie?"

Taylor stands with crossed arms while rocking back and forth, rendering him absolutely useless to us.

"Taylor, where's Scott, is he down there?" I yelled, pushing him out of the way.

"Sharpe," Screamed Robbie Garnett, who exhaustingly lays on his back, on the scorched terrain. "He, he..."

I slide on my knees to Garnett, and scream, "Where the fud is he... where's Scott?"

Robbie slowly points his sulphur-stained index finger to the sandbag wall and says, "He, he was caught by, by the skum. They, they took him away."

"How do you know they took him?" Asked the Captain, folding his arms in a now defensive stance.

"I, I heard them saying they were taking him when I was in the bunker, a few hours after the rockets struck. I was crying inside the bunker, on the stairs... but I heard absolutely everything outside fella."

"Damn." Replied the Captain.

"Scott could have sold us out... but, but he stood firm, and didn't reveal the bunker's location to the skum."

"Did they take anyone else?" Asked the Captain.

"No sir, everyone else managed to get to safety while the barrage of explosions occurred. Scott must've got trapped inside the sandbag wall. And, and that's probably how they captured him?"

"How could you understand them... they are Zakas," I asked shaking in outright fear. "Did you hear the mechanical suits of the Spectres... err, I mean the Kreeps?"

"Spectres?"

"I was meaning to say Kreeps... did you hear them?"

Funny enough, I did hear the sound of robotic mechanical limbs, and rather loud footsteps, but I can't be certain if it was the Kreeps. Some of the soldiers spoke in broken Zuntran, Sharpe. Frank, Barric's Nephew was also in contact with them too. He was screaming at Scott on the Zaka's radio. I recognised his voice immediately. The bazturd."

"Your right, some of the soldiers at the Mall spoke in broken Zuntran as well," I replied wide eyed. "What was Frank demanding of Scott?"

"Sharpe, he wanted Scott to give up our location. I heard them wrestling him into their craft when he wasn't complying to their demands."

"Captain... where do you think they've taken him?"

"Your guess is as good as mine Sharpe? They've probably transported him back to Zakataria, to work on a forced labour camp."

"Fud it," I replied clinching both fists, ever so tightly. "That bazturd Frank will kill him, I just know he will. I hope you're right Captain. He'll stand a better chance there than with that hate-filled bazturd Frank, or those fudding Spectres."

The spent men now cower from the harsh rays of the sun, that beats down heavily onto their frail bodies.

"Zenith, load the men onto the MAS that Hersh has just pulled-out."

"Affirmative captain."

"You there... what's your name?"

"That's Robbie Garnett, Captain." I said, observing Rob, who really looks worse for wear.

"Right Robbie, I need you to drive that MAS as fast as you can to the Green Zone. Don't drive in a straight line... do you hear me? I want you to zig-zag the whole darn journey. There's Zakatarian artillery units hidden deep within the Red Zone, so I need you to drive as fast as you possibly can."

"Gotcha… I, I use to drive for a living." Replied Robbie to the annoying sound of Legos, who continues to stumble about in his urine-stained pants.

"Dear oh dear… who's the happy chap, with the bottle?"

"That's General Legos, Captain."

"Really, Sharpe?"

"He's been drinking non-stop. We literally had to lock him inside his quarters, because he was threatening the personnel with pure violence. We've only just released him. We were extremely lucky to be fair."

"Why?" I asked perplexed.

"He tried to obtain a gun from the armoury, because he thought that we were conspiring to steal his whisky from him. However, luckily enough he couldn't open the armoury door with his key."

"The condition he's in, he'd have most certainly shot one of you," said the captain, shaking his head in disbelief. "Has he always liked a little tipple of drink?"

"I know... tell me about it. No, he must have hidden his dirty little secret from us," said Robbie licking his dried lips. "The C-sectors arrested Barric, Sharpe, well before the rocket attack... did you know?"

"Yep, I'm already aware."

"I heard all about Frank. What happened at the mall Sharpe?"

"Look, we don't have the time to chat Robbie, I'm sorry... perhaps I'll catch-up with you later."

"Aren't you coming with us Sharpe?"

"No, err, our transport is beyond those sandbags."

"Zenith, get that bloody General, and put him on board with the others, in case he attracts some unwanted attention from the Red Zone!"

Zenith zooms over to Legos and throws him clean over his shoulder, without the General losing a single drop of whisky from his bottle. Legos yelps and hiccups, and then proceeds to sing even louder, whilst trying to drink upside down."

"What a bloody performance." Said the captain observing his surroundings.

"I can't see your transport Sharpe," said Robbie scanning his vision across the bombed-out base. "Tell a lie... I mean, I can see one enormous crater, but there's absolutely no sign of any transportation?"

"Robbie, don't worry about us mate, we are fine."

"Yeah, but why are all your pal's dressed-up like space-cadets, Sharpe," asked Robbie bewildered by our uniforms. "The size of your friend... the black guy, is he an ex-basketball player or something?"

"Yeah, he's an ex-professional player," I replied, trying my best to change the subject. "Listen to me... where's Louie?"

"Barric, took his cat and the kittens... but I'm pretty certain he left Louie behind. Hmm, yeah, as a matter of fact he did. What league did your pal's team play in?"

"Robbie, we are in a crisis situation here pal. I don't have the time to go into the fine details of sport. Look, do me a fudding favour and give me a headcount."

"Copy that." Replied Robbie scanning the malnourished men.

"Louie... here kitty-kitty," I yelled while squinting my eyes across the base. "Come on, come out here little fella."

The destruction of the base instantly causes me to choke-up. There's absolutely no way Louie could have survived this inferno. Hopefully he scarpered back to the Green Zone when the missiles dropped.

"Wait up, Zenith!" said Hersh, peeling himself away from the MAS. "General Legos, it's me, Hersh Van Winkle... we are taking you and your men to safety. You must listen to me."

"Okay... I'm here. What's happening, and who the hell are you?" Replied General Legos, upside down and absolutely bewildered.

"It's Hersh. General, these guys need you to behave yourself, okay my friend. It's still very dangerous out here."

"Hershey, Van Winkle... my, my dear honourable friend. Did, did you like the bottle of whisky I secretly sent to you with Sharpe. It was in the darn hold-all? It was old as fud... a real bottle of fine ingredients." Asked Legos, hiccupping loudly.

"Yes... it was truly amazing. Sharpe is with us now." Said Hersh, pointing his index finger into my direction.

"I heard that he was injured," replied Legos with snot excreting from his nostrils. "Oh, that's right, I can see three of him now. Sharpe, well-well-well. Hmm, if we don't hang together..."

"We will most certainly hang apart, by our necks! Safe journey back to the Green-Zone, General Legos!" I yelled throwing a thumb up. "Load him up with the others Zenith, pronto. The darn piss head."

"For fud sake… look at the bloody state of him," said the Captain, whose eyes smoulder the large bottle of whisky, that Legos continues to drink from, like a toddler. "These poor fudders are all suffering from shellshock… I think I would have hit the drink too, to be brutally honest."

"Take your eyes off that bottle Captain… you're better than that."

"I know Sharpe, it's just that I sometimes get a severe urge to go all out. I know I shouldn't."

I reply, "Well, we need to get these men out of here, fast… so get that damn alcohol out of your darn head."

"I will Sharpe," said the captain wiping the beads of sweat from his forehead with his now, drenched flannel. "Zenith, load Robbie inside the cab. We need to get these men out of here sharpish. I'll go inside the bunker, to check for any others."

"Robbie, is that everyone accounted for?"

"Yes Sharpe," Replied Robbie, having finished his headcount. "That's everyone, well apart from your pal, Scott."

"I might just go down there anyway, just to have a browse." Said the Captain, licking his parched lips.

I begin to wonder why the captain is so adamant on wanting to go down into the bunker and instantly realise it's because of the whisky, that General Legos may still have stored away.

"No Captain, we must go now. There's no whisky down there for you," I said watching Zenith, who now helps Robbie onboard the MAS. "Let's get out of here."

Both myself and the captain head back to the cloaked Aurora and watch on as Robbie steers the MAS towards the Green-Zone, with Legos who continues to hiccup and sing inside the rear of the truck's flatbed.

"I'm really sorry about your friend (Scott) I really am," said the captain as both Zenith and Hersh join us. "Once we complete the mission, we'll have a scout around for him, although I'm not promising anything, because let's face it, they could be holding him absolutely anywhere?"

"I understand… thanks Captain."

"Guys, strap yourselves in, next stop is Zakataria," yelled the captain. "Zenith, before we head off, we will need to see to it that the General and his men return safely."

"Affirmative Captain."

"Sharpe… Hersh! Wake up, the pair of you. We need to get this krud show on the road," said the captain. "Zenith what's your status report?"

"We are positioned on the outskirts of the snowy capital of Yule, just as you ordered. The Aurora is fully cloaked, and its thrusters are all working as they should. The weapon manufacturing plant is over a mile-away from this specific location."

"What's the story with the terrain?" Asked the Captain.

"This surrounding area is exceptionally dense with vast woodland that surrounds the entire capital. According to the craft's external radar system, it's by far the safest place to set-up our electromagnetic pulse. The weapons instruction manual states that the (EMP) should be fastened down into the ground, at approximately two feet." Said Zenith holding up the base in which the device is meant to sit on.

"And hostiles?"

"Captain, the radar hasn't picked-up anything hostile… apart from various forms of wildlife dotted around, here and there. Like I said, this woodland is simply the best place to distribute the (pulse rockets) while keeping Master Sharpe safe also."

"Great. Sharpe, listen in."

"Yes Captain?" I replied eating a breakfast bar.

"I promised ma'am I would keep you safe, so I'm going to follow up on my promise and drop you off here with the (EMP). The area outside is absolutely baron in regard to any hostile activity."

"We should really stick together… no? Are you sure that there's no Spectres lurking around?"

"Sharpe, there's absolutely no sign to suggest that there's any Spectre activity, or Zakatarian military units for that matter."

"Okay, okay." I replied.

"Look, we need to kill two birds with one stone. You will set-up that device in the safety of this vast snow-covered forest, while we plant the explosives at the docks. Should you detect anything out of the ordinary, you are to hide and then inform us, but only when you are safe to do so. You got that?"

"Err… yeah, okay then."

"Sharpe, I wouldn't put you in any kind of danger," said the captain observing the onboard radar monitor. "Zenith and Hersh will place the device bang centre of this opening. Once it's in position, I want you to bury its legs into the ground to stabilise its main body, using the crank. You are to activate the timer switch and lay low, but only on my call… do you copy?"

"Sure Captain. Only on your call… right gotcha."

"Three rockets will eject one by one from the top of that device. Once airborne, they'll do the rest. The bottom of the device will become extremely hot, so please steer clear. Once detonated they'll fry all of their electronic components, nationwide."

"Why do you need to destroy the drones then? Surely the pulse will cripple them too."

"Because the drones aren't our only primary objective. The drone site is also holding vast quantities of chemicals, that they use for creating nuclear warheads. There's far too many V-twelve sites hidden throughout Zakataria, hence why we're using the (EMP)."

"How long do you think you'll be?"

"We've got our pinned place of interest already. The Dockside is just north of this position. We will destroy the drone/chemical manufacturing plant via the ocean."

"What? You mean underwater, right?"

"Correct. Hence why I need you to remain here with the (EMP) as it's far too dangerous at the Dockside. I've been informed by Ma'am that should we fail, that you are to be picked-up by Sapphire, which is another craft just like this one, however their one is fresh-off the production line."

"What?"

"Captain, Nemo Octavious and your friends, Jhita, Josh, and Yogi are all on board that craft, so you'll be in safe hands."

"Hey... you didn't say nothing about a fudding suicide mission Jason, I mean Captain?"

"It's not a suicide mission Sharpe. We've planned for absolutely every kind of scenario. All bets are covered. Me, Hersh and Zenith, will set-up the explosive charges underwater, via the pillars that hold up the various manufacturing plants above. Three charges in total should theoretically cause the whole place to crumble into the ocean... it's going to cause extreme environmental damage, but it's the only way to combat their drones, etc."

"Okay... but Captain, please be vigilant. I really don't fancy waiting around here for a hitch home."

"You'll be alright Sharpe," said the captain turning to both Zenith and Hersh. "I need both of you to carry the (EMP) to its designated position now. Sharpe, wrap-up… you'll catch your death out there."

"Copy that, Captain. Zenith, get the other side of the box." Said Hersh making his way to the large wooden box.

I'm now given a rolled-up, white padded jumpsuit from the captain and immediately tackle its tight fit, feet first, while both Zenith and Hersh exit the craft with the boxed (EMP).

"Captain, why did you hit the drink so bad? I've got to say, you look so much healthier looking now."

"Hmm, well, where shall I start?" Replied the Captain.

The captain now folds his arms and leans himself back onto the padded wall in a defensive like pose, and follows the EMP with his eyes, until they carry it out of view.

"It was a combination of things really... obviously there was the death of your mother. See, when krud hits the fan, you either swim or sink.... and I suppose, I sank."

"Yeah, but you hit the bottle well before my mother passed away?"

"Sharpe, have you ever held two point two million kredits?"

"What... Why are you asking me such a random question such as that?"

"When I was in my twenties (over twenty or so years ago) I won the Zuntran lottery, however the shopkeeper denied me of my winnings, all out of envy. He basically stole my winning ticket and threatened to destroy it."

"You've got to be kidding me Captain... okay, and pigs can fly."

I study the captain's facial expressions which instantly indicates to me that he is telling me the truth.

"Oh my, you really are telling the truth... and what did you do?" I asked stunned.

"Well, I handed him the ticket to scan it through the machine, to check my numbers. He started to behave rather peculiar, once the ticket ejected out of the machine, so I knew straightaway that the ticket was a winner, just by his behaviour. The fudder literally celebrated my lottery win right in front of me, as if it was his own."

"Didn't you try and snatch it back?"

"My hands were tied. I was limited down to various things really, I guess? I mean, he now had the ticket in his possession and threatened to destroy it, should I have lashed-out. He then went on a tyrannical pursuit to silence me, by threatening me and my family with harm. I wasn't armed with the knowledge I have now, and sort of buried it in the back of my mind, for years. I wasn't one for confrontation back then either. I was also scared that should I have informed the C-sectors, that I wouldn't have any evidence to back up my claim. The media would have found out and I would have been remembered as the idiot who lost over two million credits. It taught me a lot about the negative sides of humanity."

"So, what happened next?"

"I left the shop deflated and upset. I felt totally embarrassed and to a certain degree ashamed of myself, hence why you're the only one I've ever told."

"You've kept that bottled up for over twenty years?"

"Yes. Although I believe the whole situation was my destiny... just imagine if I had that money back then?"

"Did he cash it in?"

"No, he didn't have the bottle. It went unclaimed. Hmm, (Surinder Pal) that was his name. He knew that there would have been an investigation, by the organisation that controlled the lottery back then."

The captain now rests his back against the padded interior of the craft and continues to say, "I would have probably killed myself in a high-performance sports car anyway, or worse still, I could have been tangled-up with people who were fake... you know, those who just want to hang around with you for your kredits."

"Damn. He really did you dirty." I replied.

"No, when I look back at it, it was the right path for me. Okay, so I hit the bottle, and I guess things like that could make a good man turn bad, but look where I'm at now,

I'm in control of the Aurora, and I'm almost about to kickstart one of my wildest of dreams, dreams I had when I was a child."

"I suppose that's one way to look at it." I replied.

"See, I've always wanted to be an explorer. I want to write my own story and live my own myth."

"Fair enough Captain. Hopefully Surinder Pal, got his own bad karma handed to him."

"No, karma is merely cause and effect, Sharpe."

"What do you mean?"

"I don't believe in karma as being something that hands-out rewards and punishments, based on choices you made throughout your life. Remember, there's children out there who are suffering from various illnesses etc. Would you suggest that their pain/suffering was brought on by their own bad karma?"

"No, obviously not."

"Exactly Sharpe, hence why I think the way people view karma as being some kind of universal judgement, is just bloody wrong."

"That's an interesting way to look at it, I suppose." I replied.

"It sure is. Look at all these (new age) groups Sharpe, the ones who rhyme-on all day about good and bad karma? It's absolutely pathetic. They also try and meditate to deflect bad karma. If krud is going to happen, it's going to happen. You cannot supress it, mentally."

"But you said it was your destiny when you was robbed/denied of winning the lottery?"

"Because destiny itself is merely cause and effect. It was true (karma). Something bad did happened to me, but in the end, it ended up being a good thing."

"Hmm, you're making my brain hurt."

The captain chuckles, "Sorry Sharpe, I'm a sucker for philosophy. Anyway, once this mission is completed here, I'll head off out of this Dome, on an exploration, considered to be the greatest of achievements known to man, in the eyes of those with the same dreams. Fud the Kredits. Honestly, what doesn't kill you, will only make you stronger, buddy."

"Fair play Captain. Whatever floats your boat, I suppose. I'd love to have the opportunity to explore too."

"I don't think your aunt (Ma'am) would allow for it to happen, unfortunately."

"Well, she holds absolutely zero authority over me. I'll ultimately leave it to my own destiny."

"Fair enough," replied the captain stroking away at his stubbly chin. "Yeah, so that was my story."

"Well, kredits don't mean krud at the end of the day. Look at everyone fleeing for safety, leaving their prized possessions behind themselves. Kredits and possessions are merely ephemeral."

"Correct, however the only discrepancy I would say I still have with Surinder Pal, would be the fact that my mum suffered. If I had those kredits back then, I could have given her the quality of care that she so rightly deserved."

"I'm sorry about your mother. I remember you telling me about her illness years ago."

"It's fine, she's at peace now. You've got a lot of knowledge for a man your age Sharpe. Knowledge is extremely important."

The captain peels himself off the padded wall interior and collects his rifle that was leant up beside him, "Right, it looks like they've put the device into its position Sharpe. What's wrong... you're beginning to look slightly apprehensive?"

"No, I'm not apprehensive at all... I'm just thinking about you guys. Please take good care, Captain."

"Sharpe, we train extremely hard for such missions. We will be back here to collect you, so please don't stress-out. Remember, just press on your earlobe if you require our assistance."

"Captain, there's too many unanswered questions, that I still need answering, although I know that this isn't the right time. So, I guess I best be off then."

I spud Captain Noolan's fist and make my way to the others with my equipment. Both Hersh and Zenith sprint past me from having positioned the (EMP) and the pair look to be both on point to completing their further objectives at the dockside, because they look extremely focused.

"Good luck chaps!"

Hersh Van Winkle stops in his tracks and then turns around to me, howling like a wolf. He then lifts a clarified thumb-up into the air and proceeds to board the rear of the craft with Zenith, who is now saluting me.

The transparent Aurora slowly lifts off the ground with its rear door that closes as it ascends. It then turns and accelerates north, towards the docks. Zakatarian oak trees brush side-to-side causing clunks of snow to fall from their high branches, which in-turn crash on top of the already thick snow below.

"Well, I best be making a start." I said to myself, while watching the craft disappear into the low hanging grey clouds above.

Frozen with absolute fear, down to what may happen to my (APEX) colleagues, I instantly head toward the now, unboxed weapon. The density of the forest all around offers me exceptional peace of mind, because it appears to be absolutely free of any scarring from conflict. As a matter of fact, it's like another world altogether here.

Sudden gusts of ice-cold wind penetrate the gaps of surrounding shrubbery, creating swirls of ice that travels chaotically across the surface and into my frozen face.

"I hope they pull it off," I said out loud, while scanning my vision across the landscape. "Fud me, it sure is cold here."

Having reached the EMP, I fall to my knees and get started on its spiralled tripod legs, that are attached to the bottom of the contraption. The device itself is the same shape as an egg, and its colour is of a brilliant white, which helps it blend into the snow-covered ground.

The spiked spiral legs crunch into the layer of ice beneath the snow on each turn of the crank.

My heart begins to beat erratically because it feels like someone, or something is watching me from a distance.

An unexpected chill shoots up my spine, forcing me to squeeze my earlobe with my frost-bitten paws.

"Captain…"

"Copy Sharpe… what's up?"

"Nothing, it's just starting to get rather eerie around here."

"Hmm, something may very well be stealthing you. Keep an open eye, while you set up the device and make sure you have your pistol at the ready, with its silencer attached. It could be a wolf, although they hunt in packs… might even be a bear?

"Fud it!" I replied.

"If it's indeed a bear, whatever you do, do not run away from it. Make sure you stand your ground. They, or it, will eventually fud-off anyway. Trust me, there was no sign of any enemy units nearby. Do you copy me Sharpe?"

"Err, yeah. Copy that."

I instantly reach for the silencer, that is tucked inside my utility belt and spin it on top of the barrel of my freezing cold pistol, fast. My fingers and thumbs cramp-up with every turn, although the desperation of wanting to survive this mission, forces me to realign my mindset and forget all about the dreadful pain in my paws.

I've survived the Red Zone and those darn Teddy Boys... this is absolutely child's play compared to that. Then there's that old nutter, Psycho Bill and his Gatekeeper friends. They got served-up, nice and proper, the sadistic bazturds. Hmm, I wonder where Frank is now, the traitorous swine? But more importantly, where's Scott, I do hope he's safe and well?

I holster my pistol and proceed to crank at the tripod's legs, while simultaneously throwing my vision across the base of the distant treeline.

Having finally secured the device into place I give it one final tug. It's now ready to roll, as it's literally stuck to the ground.

"Captain... the device has been fully secured, awaiting your orders."

"Received. Sharpe, we are currently gearing-up to deploy the explosives. Move to phase two, only when you've been given the go ahead. Sit back and enjoy the tranquillity of what that area has to offer... and make sure you keep your bloody eyes-peeled for any enemy activity overhead. We will be offline in a few minutes, while we distribute our gifts to the upside-downers."

"Gotcha Captain... loud and clear. Be safe."

Do you know what? I'm so glad to be amongst a crew of gentlemen, that will happily lay down their lives for their fellow brothers/sisters and it really does bolster my vision of a positive outlook for the future. I mean, just imagine if I can wriggle my way into exploring the neighbouring domes with them? Hmm, now that would be absolutely epic, no doubt.

I wonder if this forest was the track taken by both Carol and Theodore Hammic, when she decided to leave Zakataria... just imagine if it was?

My mind's eye now creates images of what it could be like inside the adjacent domes. It throws out super realistic visions of large highly advanced civilisations, having incredible wars with each other, similar to ours. Damn, why would I want to involve myself in anymore of this kind of madness though?

Ah, man, poor Scott, I hope he's safe.

"Snap out of it and stay focused," I said out loud, while scanning my vision three hundred and sixty degrees. "What the Fud is that noise?"

The strange noise sounds as if something is scurrying underneath the snow towards me, which automatically has me spinning in all directions, with my hand now hovering over my holster. I now lay low in the snow with a heartbeat that beats like the pistons of a grizzly tank.

"Show, show yourself!" I yelled, slowly drawing my pistol from its holster.

The place now falls silent for a moment or two, and out of absolutely nowhere, a blurred (wild) looking cat launches itself at my neck, throwing me sideways. I violently land in the deep snow on my side and close my eyes for the inevitable attack, to my frozen throat.

"Louie? Louie... what the fud are you doing here?" I asked while stroking his mucky head.

Louie licks me by dragging his sandpaper tongue across my right cheek, while I try my best at standing myself up, shaking from his shock appearance.

He now manically rubs his grubby/greasy body against my immaculate boots, as I retrieve my cold pistol, that I had dropped in the snow.

Having holstered my gun away safely, I instantly smell my hands. My hands stink of krud and urine, so I decide to camouflage the awful smell, by wiping off the clumps of snow that had stuck to my jumpsuit.

"Fud, my hands are freezing. I don't understand... how is this possible? Could Louie be an illusion, brought on by this harsh weather, and why is the little fella smelling so bad?"

I kneel down to examine his body for any injuries and fail to find anything out of the ordinary. The smelly cat still dawns the makeshift harness, so I decide to have a rummage through his bulging side pockets.

"What the Fud are these?" I said to myself, as Louie leaps away from my investigation.

Ten empty Zakatarian emergency ration packs, now litter the snowy surface before my very eyes, insinuating to me that Scotty boy might still be alive, and close by.

I frantically scurry to collect the shiny foil wrappers, because I wouldn't want them to attract any unwanted attention from above.

The EMP takes Louie's attention away from me until I ask, "Where's Scott?"

Louie spins and jumps into the direction of the tree line to my right, and then begins to move out like a little bouncing rabbit.

I follow the dirty yellow trail in the snow, left behind by the smelly cat and eventually make it to the edge of the thick forest, "Is Scott in here Louie? Where is he little fella? This is fudding crazy?"

I pause to take a look at the distance of the EMP.

"Hmm, I should really wait at the (EMP) until the captain is back online," I said to myself, continuing to look at the weapon in the distance. "But I need to see if Scott's being held captive? Fud it, I've got to check it out."

The clever cat now leads me to a gap in a large thorn bush, which has got just enough room for me to squeeze my body through, without being torn apart by its razor-sharp spikes. Heat, along with the putrid smell of piss and krud emits from an opened circular vent, that appears to lead down into some sort of shaft, which is just big enough for myself to venture into.

"Fud it. My hands... I can actually feel my hands? Damn, it sure is hot down here. That smell is absolutely atrocious... I wonder where it's coming from?"

Beads of sweat now trickle down my forehead and neck, making the white jumpsuit stick to my now saturated armour. The suit must come off, as it's now beginning to restrict my movement.

I immediately take it off and tuck the rolled-up suit behind some sort of generator, that's attached to the squared walls inside the extended tunnel.

"Hmm, I wonder what this generator is being used for?"

Having readjusted my (Howling Wolves) body armour, I cautiously move forward into the unknown. The struggling bulbs attached to the walls inside, both buzz and flicker as I pass them.

"What the fud is this place? Louie, take me directly to Scott."

Sliding from wall to wall I make it to a bend that Louie now stealthy enters around. I follow the cat's tail and can now hear a faint humming sound, that sounds as if it's coming from deeper down the partially lit hallway.

"Louie… Louie, here kitty-kitty." Said the familiar voice of Scott, from inside an opened doorway, coming up on my right side.

Louie cautiously enters into the grotty doorway of the room, to the sound of heavy rattling shackles. However, I on the other hand hold back, due to the emotions coursing through my mind, of not knowing Scott's overall condition.

My heart feels like it's about to explode, from out of my parched throat.

"Psst…"

"Who, who's that?" Asked Scott bewildered.

"Scott… it's me, Paul Sharpe." I replied trying my best to compose myself, due to the grotesque stench that lingers throughout the hallway.

Fear now rips straight through me.

"Voices, there just voices. I don't want to die down here. Although, I know I'm already dead. I'm awfully glad I've got you down here with me, Louie. I don't know where I would be without you?"

"Scott, it's me," I quietly said, turning my head from right to left continually, like a raving lunatic. "Listen up… is there anyone expected to arrive down here? I need to know what I'm up against, before I enter into this darn room, buddy?"

"Ah, nothing but wild voices yet again, playing darn crazy tricks on my unstable mind… I just want my mum.

Whenever I hear these voices, I half-die." Replied Scott, crying.

Having failed at communicating with a now sobbing Scott, I take one enormous deep breath of the devilish scent, that ripples out from the room, that Scott has so tragically been imprisoned inside of. I now exhale the dank stench and can now feel my heart rate lower.

Scott hoarsely cries as I enter the room and then manically rubs soot from his eyes, so that he can get a clearer view of me.

"No way... just figments of my imagination. It's an illusion of my old friend, Paul Sharpe."

"Cut it out Scott. Listen-in, Louie directed me to you... okay. You must help me out here pal. Are you expecting any guards to come and check in on you?"

"Sharpe, it really is you... but how did you know I was here?"

"Look, we haven't got the time to piss around. I need to know who checks up on you? How many units are there?"

"Frank the wank is here… you've got to be careful, because he, he normally checks-in on me every now and then. I'm the only surviving Zuntran. They killed them all, Sharpe. The bazturds literally took them, and killed them in that hallway behind you," cried Scott sniffing. "Frank believes he can exchange me for Psycho Bill. He's off his fudding darn head."

"Oh, does he now?" I said, turning my head outside the doorway to observe the long trail of blood further up the hall, to my right. "He's a fudding sick man and a dead one at that. Do you keep a tab on his visits?"

"I haven't seen daylight for ages. I don't keep tabs… he comes in, throws urine and krud all over me, and then casually goes back out the door at the end of the hall, to the right. Louie has been bringing me ration packs, by using the various vents. The slippery cat managed to sneak on board their chopper, after they attacked our base. Hey, you'll no doubt hear Frank, because he needs to unlock the door to enter into the hall outside."

"Fantastic. What is this place?"

"Well, Goth is the mastermind. This is where they, himself and Frank etc, assemble the major components used for their hypersonic missiles. They've even got a new drone production line, lower down in the facility. They transferred the production line from the Docks, to here."

"Fud... you never mentioned anything about Goth... and the production lines?" I asked gulping.

"Goth wants me dead. Frank has saved my bacon from him a number of times. He travels in a wheelchair, yet he sometimes swings on those poles attached to the ceiling behind you. He's stealthy as fud Sharpe, and never makes a single noise to alert me of his presence. But Louie never misses a thing... do you Louie?" Said Scott stroking the cat.

"What the fud?" I replied startled.

"Honestly Sharpe, the guy is a freak of nature... he literally swings like a chimpanzee on those rails above your head. He apparently lost his legs, while experimenting with explosives. A very dangerous man. We, we will need to steer clear of him."

"You mentioned the docks? Please explain?"

"The equipment at the dockside, used to make weapons, has been moved to here. A few Zuntran prisoners (who were working here before I arrived) told me that they were forced to move chemicals, machinery etc, before they succumbed to their perilous end. Frank chopped their fudding heads off, the poor bazturds."

"Are you sure there isn't any more prisoners?"

"No, he murdered them all."

"Right, I need to inform the others immediately."

"Others? No, you need to get me the fud out of here, sharpish. You can't leave me here with these lunatics, aye?"

"I'm not going anywhere."

I press onto my earlobe, "Captain, do you copy over?"

"Sharpe, loud and clear. We are all set. Charges have been deployed. No casualties. Detonation will commence very soon. How is it at your end? Is the device stable enough for ejection? Listen, your tracker appears to have gone wayward... are you okay?"

"Captain... we have won the lottery, my friend," I said peering down the hall. "The darn Docks is a decoy... you literally dumped me on top of a new V-twelve missile/drone etc, development site."

"Sharpe. What are you talking about?"

"Listen to me Captain. They also have the chemicals stored here, the ones we need to destroy. The dockside is a fudding decoy, for crying out loud. I found Scott, via Louie. I'm here with him now. Abort the Docks and bring some explosives to my location, using my tracker, hurry. My tracker isn't wayward, its working just fine... do you copy over?"

"Err, what on this Flat Earth are you going on about, Sharpe?"

"Please Captain, you must hurry."

"You was given strict orders to maintain that (EMP) Sharpe. You may land yourself in some serious trouble now... are you feeling, okay?"

"Fudding listen to me now... abort the bloody Docks and get to this underground location."

"Copy... we're on our way."

The seriousness in my voice has finally swayed the captain... I just hope he hurries himself though, because this is absolutely dire.

I turn to Scott flustered, "Right, we need to break those shackles. Now, on my call, I'll need you to look the other way, while I shoot the shackle's main link."

Drawing my pistol downwards, I line-up my aim, "Three, two, one... now!"

My pistol kicks back, producing a silent but effective thud that totally obliterates the link, freeing Scott from his trauma.

"I'll need you to remain exactly where you are though. Stay positioned as if you're still chained-up, until help arrives."

"No… Goth! He's behind you Sharpe!" Cried Scott.

"Where?"

Araqia's Finest

An explosion of both shock and anger erupts deep inside of me, as I apprehensively turn around to face the maniac.

Goth swings and lunges himself violently at my being, from the metal rail that he utilises to travel. Having catapulted himself with his enormous outstretched muscular arms, the greasy/oily bazturd then impacts me and clings on to my neck with his left arm, almost like a boa constrictor. Aiming his interest onto my gun he instantly knocks it clean-out of my grasp with his free hand, sending it flying into the dirt.

"Scott, do something!"

Goth now begins to punch the side of my face-in with his right fist, forcing me to stoop my head from his granite knuckles. His strikes are precise and immediately have me struggling to breathe.

I grab his slippery right wrist (with my right hand) and try my utmost best to buffer his hits, but his strength is out of this world, especially for someone who's disabled. It's almost like the power of his missing lower limbs have somewhat transferred to his upper body, because I'm finding it extremely difficult to shake the bazturd off.

"Scott... get my pistol!" I screamed, slipping and sliding in the krud.

I take the gamble and tense-up for more inevitable strikes to the head, while I scan the floor for my gun. Having found my feet, I also find my gun and decide to kick the pistol into Scott's direction.

Goth spots the pistol sliding in the piss and readies his aim at Scott's neck. He tries to leap into Scott's direction, by using me as his launchpad, although I deflect his new target by forcibly clutching onto his left arm. Goth's failed launch sees him spin back around me, clutching my neck yet again. His greasy long hair dangles over my shoulder armour and his rancid breath stinks of both, cigarettes and coffee.

"Florian-Glotan!" Yelled Goth, trying his best to put me into a headlock.

"Scott… hurry up and shoot the bazturd!"

"Okay!" cried Scott, scurrying in the sludge. "Don't let go of him."

"Florian-Glotan! Florian-Glotan!" Screamed Goth.

Scott's grimy outstretched fingers aim directly for the pistol, that now lays in a pool of urine, a metre or so in front of him. His shackles both cling and clang as he crawls.

"Hurry!" I cried.

Scott successfully grabs hold of its wooden handle grip and lifts the dripping gun upwards, however he now struggles to get a clear shot, down to us both grappling with each other.

"Now… light him up!"

"I can't Sharpe, I might hit you!"

I look right and take another hit, that creates a crunching sound, just under my right eye-socket.

Out of sheer luck I realign my vision and spot a sharp protruding metal fixing, a foot above waist height, which connects to the hanging shackles. Using all my core strength I both parry and throw myself backwards into the direction of the fixing, and successfully impale the brute onto the wall. I then use the remaining smidgen of energy I have left, to lift the sadistic fudder upwards, causing the parasite to squeal in extreme agony.

Goth now sticks to the wall from having his spine wreaked on the six-inch fitting and pleads for me to detach him by gesturing with his hands.

Having peeled myself away from his stinking spent body and now hanging arms, I take my time to catch my breath, while supporting my cheekbone from the shots sustained from his furious right hand.

"Florian-Glotan!" Screamed Goth, as he hangs on the wall like a hunter's trophy.

I splash my knee pads into the sludge with my head in my hands, brought on by the flurry of ferocious punches. Blood gushes out from my right eye creating a metal taste that uninvitingly enters into the sides of my mouth.

Straightening myself out has now become an impossible task, because my head is pulsating, and feels as if my brain is about to pop out from my ears.

"Sharpe, we must go!" Yelled Scott.

"Florian-Glotan!"

"Scott... shut him up! Shoot the fudder!"

The suppressed slugs rip straight through the side of Goth's torso, stapling him to the murky wall, even more so.

"You okay Sharpe?" Panicky asked Scott, as I observe Goth's blood and cerebral spinal fluid, which runs down the wall that he so peacefully hangs from.

"I'll survive. What was he saying?" I asked.

"Goth wasn't like the run-of-the-mill Zakatarian, who speaks with the universal tongue. He spoke in old Zaka. He was crying out for Frank to help him. Frank may very well have heard him though. We must go now Sharpe."

"Hang on! I've lost my earpiece. It's what they'll use to track our location. It must have flew out during the attack. Fud it... they may have trouble finding us now?"

Scott manically searches for the white coloured earpiece in the sludge, "fud the thing... let's go."

"Okay... okay," I replied dazed and confused. "Louie, go outside and lead my friends here... go!"

The cat darts out from cowering behind Scott and immediately exits the room towards the tunnel that leads out to the thorn bush.

"Sharpe... come on we've got to get out of here."

"Scott, help me up. I've just had my face smashed-in... I'm struggling here."

The clanging of keys emits from down the hall.

"Fud it… it's Frank," yelled Scott who now crawls back to his corner, rocking back and forth. "He may have heard all of the commotion. Sharpe, hide yourself in the shadow… right there, in the corner of the room. He'll not see you… please hurry."

"He's going to see the dead body though," I replied, as Frank clangs his bunch of keys against the locking mechanism of the door. "You'll have to shoot him, because I'm punch drunk. Honestly, I can hardly see out of my eyes."

Scott conceals my pistol underneath his thigh but maintains a tight grip on its handle.

"Goth, what are you doing up here? The processing computer for the warheads are coming up as non-functional? They're beginning to spew-out fumes from the chemical converter system," yelled Frank, whose footsteps draw nearer-and-nearer to the dimly lit room. "Goth… where are you?"

I press my sweaty back up-against the slimy brick wall and draw-in an enormous deep breath of damp air, to help alleviate my erratic nerves. The air in the room is stagnant and tastes of krud, and urine, to the point that I want to puke-out a lung.

"Goth... I know you're up here; your wheelchair is outside! You promised me that you wouldn't enter this part of the complex? If you've touched my prisoner," warned Frank, who now draws out his gun. "You'll leave me no choice... urgh!"

Frank enters the room and instantly recoils from seeing Goth's inanimate body, stuck to the wall, "What-what the fud?"

"He-he... he tried to kill me Frank," stammered Scott. "Goth left me with no other option, but to kill him. I did it because I want to help you free Psycho Bill."

"This isn't your doing. Besides, you're cuffed, and Goth would have torn you to shreds. Somebody has been inside here?" Remarked Frank, studying the bloodied torso.

"It was me," replied Scott, rocking back and forth. "I choked him with my chains."

"Goth had all the codes for the warheads... damn. The system needs to be overridden, otherwise the fumes will sweep through the site," said Frank, turning his attention to Scott. "He's been bloody shot... who's been in here?"

I instantly peel myself off the wall and target Frank, who instantly clicks back the hammer-pin of his silver revolver.

"Paul Sharpe!" Cried Frank.

Startled by my violent presence he immediately pulls the trigger; however my tight grasp of his gun's long barrel manages to steer the round clear from Scott, who now draws my pistol upwards. He aims my (PPK) at Frank, yet due to us tussling around, he refrains from firing it.

"Scott! Shoot him!"

"Sharpe, I can't get a clear shot!"

The heat of Frank's barrel burns my palms, but I stay focused, because I know what he is capable of doing.

"It's you," screamed Frank, yanking away at his gun. "You cannot win!"

My ears are now ringing out in pain from the random round, yet I ignore it, as it's now a fight for survival.

I work my hands towards the trigger, and grip hold of the body of his revolver, using all of my bodyweight. Shuffling my feet to the right I proceed to headbutt Frank, using the side of my head (the side that was undamaged by the earlier attack) however, he overpowers me by pushing his thumbnail clean into my busted eye.

Panicked, and in extreme pain, I feel around my eyeball to see if it's still attached to its socket, "My eye... you bazturd!"

"Don't you get it, you red-eyed fudder, you cannot win!" Screamed Frank, throwing me to the ground besides Scott, who out of sheer fright from my appearance, bottles firing the pistol.

"Let him have it," I yelped, as Scott drops the barrel. "I didn't mean give him my gun... I meant light the fudder-up!"

"Don't listen to him Scott! Drop the gun," exclaimed Frank. "Sharpe… didn't you learn nothing at the Red Zone?"

"You bazturd… you killed the Screaming Hawks unit."

"They deserved all they got. Funnily enough, they thought I was you, up until I murdered them!" Bellowed Frank now laughing like a twisted hyena.

"You're not going to get away with this!"

"Oh, shut up Sharpe. If only you could see how pathetic you look now. I should have brought that gold cased mirror, so you could see yourself. That's right, you know… the one I had stolen off you back at the stronghold. Look at you, all sprawled-out on the floor, just like you were at Old Islington Mall."

"You are nothing but a dirty murderous, thieving bazturd."

"Shut it, Sharpe! Who's here with you?" cried Frank. "Where's the rest of the Howling Wolves?"

"I'm alone!"

"Liar... I know they're here. Give me their location now, or I'll kill the pair of you!" Snarled Frank, aiming his gun at Scott's head.

"Scott, shoot the bazturd... he needs us as bartering chips, so that he can free that nut job, Bill."

"He hasn't got the minerals... he's a fraggle, just like you!" yelled Frank, brandishing his (snake and dagger) neck tattoo. "Why do you think you can come in here, like some fake-ass superhero... why do you persist, hey... why do you fudding persist?"

Battered, bruised and bleeding heavily I watch on as Scott slowly lowers my pistol.

I then look up at Frank and quietly reply, "Because I choose too."

From out of absolutely nowhere, Louie the cat springs-up and attacks Frank from behind. Frank aimlessly thrashes his arms around, in the hope that the screaming cat will scarper. Having failed in doing so, he blindly fires his gun upwards, which makes Louie even more vicious. One of the rounds strikes the cat's armoured harness, forcefully jolting him, yet the cat miraculously clings onto Frank's skin, spitting and screaming.

"Get him Louie," yelled Scott. "Rip his fudding face-off!"

Louie embeds his claws deep into Frank's spiteful, murderous face, causing him to stumble around like an old drunkard. The screaming cat then targets Frank's throat, with his razor-sharp teeth and violently mauls at his Adam's apple.

Frank indiscriminately fires his revolver yet again, narrowly missing the cat's head and continues to both choke, and scream, "Argh… little bazturd! Get him off me!"

"He's out of rounds," I cried, observing Frank's slashed face. "Scott, light him up… but watch out for Louie!"

Scott now readjusts his aim and fires my pistol, hitting Frank clean in the chest with four brutal shots, that sends him falling backwards, and out into the hallway.

"Take that you horrible bazturd." Exclaimed Scott, as the crying cat hurtles in mid-air, aiming his bloodstained claws for the ceiling's rails.

The hallway suddenly lights up like a disco with various suppressed rounds, presumably coming from my (APEX) colleagues. Menacing slugs cut Frank's flesh-off, in large clumps, as his lifeless body hits the hallway wall, opposite our room. Frank slides down the wall staring at us, as the rounds fall silent.

Louie now hangs from Goth's handrail from having avoided the blistering rounds below, and then lands unscathed on top of Frank's inanimate body, that's absolutely riddled with smoking holes.

"Is that you Captain?" I loudly hollered, watching the clumps of sizzling flesh.

The cat casually sits on Frank's ripped open chest and proceeds to clean-off the blood from his front paws.

"Sharpe, it's us. Your tracker went offline. I can't believe it... your cat actually directed us here." Replied the Captain, brushing Louie off to check Frank's pulse.

"I wouldn't bother Captain... Frank's smoking."

"Your right Sharpe, he's toast. I'm just taking his (DNA) swab. The authorities will want to register his death, back at Region-Five."

"Scott, Louie has literally saved our lives... the courageous Pit-Fighter, hey."

"The courageous Pit-Fighter, who single-handedly killed five thousand Zakatarians." Chuckled Scott, passing me my pistol.

"What's so funny lads?"

"Ah, it's a private joke Captain... you wouldn't understand."

"Right, okay... I've got his sample." Said the Captain, with Louie walking in and out of his legs.

"Great. Err, Captain, we are both injured," I replied while clambering up onto my feet. "One of you will need to cover the door at the end of the hall. There could very well be more enemy units on their way up to our location."

"Your right eye looks awful Sharpe, but don't worry... you're both in safe hands now."

Scott cries, "Sharpe, tell him we've got to go now."

"Relax, Hersh is keeping watch on that door as we speak. What a bloody performance hey? What the fud has happened in here, there's blood and gore everywhere?" Asked the Captain, who studies Goth's body like an exhibit piece in a museum.

"He was their mastermind, in regard to explosives and nuclear warheads etc." Replied Scott sobbing.

"Hmm, Zull Gothberg, better known as Goth the legless. He has been off our radar for many years. We really have won the lottery, pal. Why is his body up there though?"

"He wanted to hang out with us and rudely overstayed his welcome," I replied, chuckling. "Listen Captain, we need to rig this place up with explosives."

"Hersh has already placed a number of charges throughout the hallway, they should be suffice. The escaping fumes will ignite the place anyway. I can't believe it hasn't gone up already to be fair, especially with the potent smell of gunpowder, chemicals etc."

"Frank mentioned something about a leak coming out from the chemical converter system?"

"That doesn't sound too good Sharpe. Right, we need to get the pair of you out of here, but I'll need to swab Goth first."

The captain collects the sample of Goth's blood and then covers our backs as we exit the dungeon.

"Come on… let's go," said the captain with his pistol aimed at the door.

Turning left, we safely make it around the main bend in the hallway, with Louie, who jumps into my arms as we scarper. We now jog to Hersh, who forces both me and Scott to take a sip of his fine whisky from his green hip flask.

"That should calm your nerves men," said Hersh nearing to the generator. "Let's go!"

"Scott, throw my jumpsuit on... I hid it behind this generator. You can't go outside half-naked. It's fudding freezing out there."

"No... I've rigged that generator with high explosives! Steer well clear!" yelled Hersh, who points his pistol to the exit. "Go!"

Having made it out of the thorn bush and clear of the tree line we sprint toward Zenith, who defensively stands armed with a machine gun, beside the Aurora's rear ramp.

The captain screams, "Go-go-go!"

"Sharpe... It's a fudding Kreeper!" Yelled Scott who struggles to keep up, down to his knackered knees and half naked body.

"It's not... look I'll explain everything to you once we are safely on board. Now hurry the fud up!"

Whistling Zakatarian rounds whizz pass us as we zig-zag our way to the Aurora.

Hersh suddenly directs his attention to the thirty metre away (EMP) and peels himself away from us. He runs to the right and then slides in the snow. Lifting the cover of the control panel, he frantically punches the required information into the device.

Zenith randomly opens fire at the tree line and sees to it that we are safely on board, by covering us with his enormous frame.

"Captain, the (EMP) is activated!" Cried Hersh, who now ducks from the random rounds being fired from the enemy, that remain hidden deep inside the snow-covered woodland.

"Hurry… get on board! The Zakas are spilling out from the shaft behind that thorn bush!"

"I can't Captain. I must see to it that the rockets eject," replied Hersh. "We have to complete the mission. They may have more hidden sites… go!"

"No… he's not going to make it back!" I cried out from the safety of the armoured Aurora.

The captain pauses on the steps of the ramp and pulls his hair out in utter frustration. He then bites his fist, cursing at the surrounding woodland that's lighting up with machine-gun fire.

"Get her off the ground now!" Screamed Hersh, who now holds up the detonation switch for the explosives, that he had planted inside the hallway.

"Zenith! Get on board and lift-her-up!" Yelped the Captain.

Zenith races past us and follows on with his orders, by safely storing his machine gun on the rack. He then heads himself to the controls and spins on the captain's seat, firing-up the thrusters.

"Hold on to something, fast," yelled Zenith. "You may want to strap yourselves in!"

The craft now lifts off at full thrust, blowing the snow underneath outwardly, which instantly reveals the rocky surface below us.

"Captain, the surface below looks extremely fragile." Said Zenith, staring at the craft's main monitor screen.

Hersh stares up at me and clicks the switch, with a smile from ear-to-ear.

"Boom"

Nesting birds flee the trees in their hundreds from all directions, totally blocking-out the sunlight, that's now creeping out of the clouds.

The ground rumbles and cracks from the enormous underground explosions, causing various trees to now lean and fall onto the snow-covered ground below.

"Sharpe, strap yourself in!" Cried the Captain.

"No! We need to save Hersh!" I yelped, observing Hersh from the opened rear door of the craft.

Countless of felled trees have now created large plumes of snow that travels outwardly across the large opening.

The place falls eerily silent along with the rounds of the enemy… until all hell breaks loose. The tree line is now non-existent, because the force of the underground explosions have made the surrounding ground collapse in on itself, taking the heavy snow along with it.

"We need to get out of here!" Cried Scott, locking himself into the rear passenger chair, with smelly Louie, who frantically seeks refuge under his seat.

I scream at the top of my lungs, "Hersh, hurry!"

The rear door slowly closes, causing yet another pang of fear to erupt inside my stomach.

"We need to retrieve Hersh... keep the door open Captain!"

"We can't override it Sharpe... the door closes-up automatically."

"No!" I screamed.

Hersh struggles to stand up from the constant rumbles and shakes of the precarious ground, but heroically maintains the stability of the (EMP) by kneeling and hugging the large egg-shaped weapon.

The lid of the contraption now opens up with its three rockets that protrude upwards. Smoke and then fire explodes from its underside, catapulting the rockets into the air, one by one. They whistle upwards and out of sight from Hersh, who now brushes-off the flames from his chest, that had developed from the eruption of the three rocket's boosters.

Zenith bends his neck around to the rear of the craft, "Rockets are on course Captain, one-hundred-feet and climbing. The ground below us is very unstable... we may lose Hersh."

The rear door seals shut, so I immediately run to the adjacent observation window, to observe Hersh, whose legs wobble, down to the enormous cracks that are now surrounding his position.

The earth below us now snaps in half, and slowly crumbles into the abyss.

Hersh looks up at me and takes one last swig of whisky, and then launches it into the fiery pit, that rages around him. His flask explodes due to its flammable contents. Reaching for the pendant of his daughter, that was tucked behind his chest plate, he draws it close to his moustache and kisses her tiny little photo.

My heart now sinks, as I watch him howling like a wolf.

"He knows his ghastly circle of suffering is drawing to an end." I said to myself, pressing my burnt bloody palm onto the window, to say my farewells.

Scott now cries for his mother.

"The pulse has been deployed Captain, at approximately four hundred feet. According to my calculations, the weapons should have already crippled their computer systems (nationwide). I'll update you as soon as I know more."

"Fine... Zenith, steer us clear of any potential danger. These explosions are far too close for comfort."

Zenith moves us out, down to the turbulence caused by the random blasts/shockwaves, etc.

The cracks between the rocky surface below us, looks like rivers of fiery veins, that are beginning to throw-up plumes of black smoke and thunderous flames.

We now fly over Hersh who continues to howl on the only surviving ledge, and watch on in agony, as the ground beneath him slowly swallows him up.

"No!" I exclaimed, with tears of blood gushing out of my eyes.

Choked and shocked, the captain turns away from the observation window and quietly says, "Sharpe... sit down and buckle-up pal. I'm so sorry... look, it is what it is. Hersh was most definitely, Araqia's finest."

I continue to watch out the window from the safety of my seat. An enormous mushroom cloud rises-up from Hersh's resting place, off in the distance, as we accelerate back to Region-Five.

Nobody says a single word the whole darn journey home, apart from the odd cough here and there. The silence is deafening, deafening to the point that I close my weeping eyes and fall asleep to the therapeutic hum of the Aurora's thrusters.

Left Hand Path

It has been approximately two weeks since we completed (Operation Deep freeze) and I'd openly admit, it's been hard to shake off those traumatic memories. Visions of Hersh's last moments have been replaying themselves over-and-over again in my mind's eye, to the point that I felt like I needed to reach-out.

Finding a way to articulate myself around the subject was the hardest part, because I have never really been the one to open myself up like that. The medic at Region-Five suggested that I should document my thoughts/feelings into a journal, that she so kindly gifted to me... along with her contact number, should I need a shoulder to cry on. She seems like a really pleasant lady and her advice was absolutely spot on, as I haven't left my journal alone.

I started to write about my experiences that I had at an early age, up until now and literally haven't put the pen down.

"Sharpe. Ma'am will see you shortly," said Andy, popping his head out the large Chamber doors, that leads to Ma'am's quarters. "Look, I'm really sorry about what happened in the chamber, a few weeks back, and I'm also sorry about your pal, the one who lost his life in Zakataria."

"Andy... don't worry. You're a member of Ma'am's security staff, so I totally understand. As for Hersh... well, he's at peace now."

"Just wanted to pass on my condolences. Err, why don't you wait in the hallway? It's far warmer in there, than this freezing cold chamber."

"The quietness of this chamber allows me to think. Besides, that hallway is far too busy."

"So, what's that you're reading?"

"I'm not reading Andy, I'm writing."

"Oh, writing, hey. Reading and writing bore me to death. Here, I managed to bench press two-hundred- and ten-kilograms last night. I only done ten reps though, but I'm increasing the weight, all down to my specialised dietary plan. Perhaps you could tag along with me one day? I could do with a spotter."

"Cor, are you entering into the Olympics or something?"

"Very funny... look, have a think about it and get back to me. Your height/frame could pack on some serious muscle. Talking of muscle, they'll be hosting the Grayson Furious fight in here soon. He's apparently fighting that Torokian guy, err, what's his name again? That's it, Chiroza. I'll be ringside. Maybe you can join me?"

"I'll sleep on it." I replied, opening my journal.

"Okay then... hmm, I'll go in and check, to see if she's free to see you. Remember, have a think about what I said?"

"Thanks Andy." I replied, putting my pen to paper.

This section of Region Five was very busy last week. The chamber had hosted various gatherings, which for the majority of the time remained a (closed door policy) meaning I didn't get an invite. Although, information has been trickling out and apparently the Southern Alliance has accelerated its capture of the Ice Rim's other regions.

For the past week I've found refuge and solitude in the chamber, as it's extremely quiet, down to the now dwindling meetings/events. It's been like an inner sanctum.

Ma'am (my aunt) has been very distant, but I guess it's because she's bogged down with everything that's going on. It's strange really, because there's times when I feel like she's trying to avoid me. It may very well be the case that I remind her of my mother, or that she may be unwell, and hiding it from me? Who knows?

Now, I can't be certain, but I feel like this place has got many hidden secrets, secrets that I'm eager to reveal. I accidentally fell asleep in here the other night, on one of the Chamber's many luxurious sofas and was awoken by Ma'am who was totally unaware of my presence. She was walking and talking behind three members of staff, who appeared to have been pushing a hospital bed into the hallway of her quarters. Now, I'm not sure if there was anyone in the bed, because my eyes were glued together with sleep, but it really did make me wonder at the time, in regard to why she would need a hospital bed? Perhaps she's unwell and preparing for it?

On our arrival back to Region Five, Scott was immediately rushed into the military's intensive care unit, while I waited around in its accident and emergency department, for some well needed stitches to my right eyebrow and cheekbone.

My eye has healed up considerably well. All that remains now is the thick stitches that are soon to be pruned.

I've not seen or heard from Scott since (Operation Deep Freeze) however, I've been inundated from the captain, who has assured me that he is doing just fine. Apparently both Scott and Taylor are recovering on the same ward, which is located on the lower level of Region-Five, with Louie as company. Man, I can't wait to see them again.

General Legos and his (merry men) successfully made it back to the Green Zone unscathed from the Zakatarian artillery, however they've now been split-up into various mobile Z-six divisions, across the north section of Hammic's Walls, while the General himself gets the well needed support for his alcoholism, here at Region-Five.

Robbie Garnett and Maloney have apparently been moved into an ammunition logistics unit, to help distribute the rounds to each of the guns. I just hope they're safe and well.

The very next day, I was interviewed by the C-sectors and based on my evidence, and character reference of General Barric, they've released him without charge, which is nice to know, as it was Frank who chose to align himself with the enemy. Just imagine if I didn't have that conversation with General Barric, before I watched, Zuntra and its struggle? The chat we had appears to have saved his life.

Frank and Goth's (DNA) samples were entered into the Zuntran data base, causing the news of their deaths to ripple throughout our land. According to the Captain, Zakatarian troops are now falling back to their homeland, to help preserve their receding munitions, just in case we invade. He also told me that their people and military personnel are starting to revolt against their elites, down to their living conditions.

I must say, it really is beginning to bore the life out of me here. I've since handed in my application to join Captain Noolan, Zenith and Eric Hughes, on their journey to (Zeno Four.) Eric Hughes was drafted-in due to the tragic death of Hersh, but I don't think he's ready, to be honest. I don't mean to be bad on the guy, but I feel like he's got a lot to learn. He could probably start off, by peeling away at his rather large ego, because he comes across as someone who's extremely self-absorbed.

The other day (Hughes) was doing backflips out of the rear door of the Aurora. I only told him to be careful, as he may injure his back etc, and he took it totally the wrong way. I can't be bothered with people like that. The guy is an absolute moron.

The captain decided to halt the trip to (Zeno-Four) due to the much-needed modifications to the Aurora. The passing of Hersh Van Winkle, prompted both the captain and the engineers to modify the rear doors of both Aurora, and Sapphire, so that an unnecessary death doesn't occur again. Apparently, they're also mounting a Z-four styled turret at the rear end of each craft, to bolster their defence from rear end assaults.

"Damn, I've been waiting here for ages," I said to myself, as the door to the Chambers entrance opens. "Fudding piss takers."

Captain Noolan enters the Chamber from the hall, that leads to the cargo hold, "Who's a piss taker?"

"I wasn't talking to you... I was talking about this lot," I said, gesturing to Ma'am Quarters with my head.

"Talking to yourself hey… probably brought on by the slaps you sustained from both Goth and Frank. Those cuts around your eye weren't worth a stitch."

"Very funny (Captain krud pants) … not."

"I don't know why you're bothering Sharpe. She's not going to let you come with us."

"Look, she has absolute zero control over me," I replied, as both the Captain and Zenith draw nearer to the doors that travels to Ma'am's quarters. "Anyway… stop being so damn negative."

"Hello, Master Sharpe."

"Hi Zenith, nice shades."

"Why… thank you Master Sharpe. The captain bought them for me. He accidentally sat on my other ones and broke a lens."

"He has a tendency of going around, breaking things, especially people's hopes and dreams."

"Now come on Sharpe, that's a little bit below the belt."

"Yeah, and so was your remark about my eye. It's true… what are you doing to reinforce my dreams? Fudding nothing whatsoever. You prance around like a (top gun) pilot, you and your boyfriend there. And as for that Hughes fella, he hasn't got the minerals. Yet you continue to big-him-up like he's some kind of God."

"Hey, it's ultimately down to Ma'am and Alex Pale etc, to give the green light. I'm powerless. Hughes has been highly recommended by the Southern Alliance. Okay, so he loves himself…"

"What a load of horse krud. What about me, locating and taking down the hypersonic missile threat," I replied while going back to writing. "Anyway, I'm busy… goodbye."

The captain crosses his arms and says, "It's out of my hands. Your heroism hasn't gone unnoticed though. I can assure you now that they'll find something here within this Ice Wall… hmm, like the C-sectors, or something along those lines. Anyhow, you wouldn't have located the site if it wasn't for your cat?"

"Your right, it wasn't just me who destroyed their weapons facility. It was a joint effort by all involved, hence why I think Hughes isn't ready. The C-sector are a bunch of snobby, jobs worths and you know it. I'd rather go back into the military."

"You don't mean that." Said the Captain.

"I bloody do," I replied going back to my journal. "I'm busy… bye-bye and take the pavement slab with you."

"That's not a nice thing to say about Zenith."

"I was saying bye to Zenith, not you."

"Very funny," replied the captain, flustered. "Maybe we can enter the Chamber and start over again. I'm sorry."

"Captain, you're blocking my light source, can you please remove yourself from my being?"

"Oh, so you're a writer now? A man of many talents. I wish I could take you Sharpe, I really do, but your mother… err, I mean Ma'am, isn't going to let you go."

I drop my pen into my journal and close it, "Hold up… you just referred to my aunt (Ma'am) as being my mother?"

"No-no, I didn't. I said Ma'am."

"Liar! Why are you lying? You just called Ma'am, my mother?"

The captain crumbles and now remains silent.

"I've managed to upgrade both your Pit Fighter trench coat and your pistol Master Sharpe. I've added armour to your jacket's shoulders, and I've even extended your pistol's barrel. This should now increase both accuracy, and power."

"Don't try and change the subject Zenith. Anyway, what's the point of making such upgrades, if I'm to remain in this dump?"

"Come on Sharpe, don't be like this." Said the Captain, shaking his head.

"Right, that's it… I've had enough of being lied to. Jason, you better move from me now. You are not my Captain, you're nothing but a bone-faced liar. Don't piss on me and tell me it's raining. I know for a fact that you're hiding something from me!"

"Sharpe, let me explain!"

"Master Sharpe, please let the captain explain."

"Master hey? So, who do you serve, Zenith? Me, or the captain?"

"Why, you obviously Master. Ma'am has programmed me to serve and protect you at all costs."

"Zenith, I demand you to hold the captain under arrest."

"Affirmative master Sharpe."

Zenith instantly grabs hold of Jason's wrists and wrestles them up behind his back.

"Wow!" I exclaimed.

"No way… this is madness," exclaimed the captain. "Sharpe stop this right now. You don't know what you are doing."

"I know exactly what I'm doing… it's called, cause and effect, or better still, my own destiny/karma."

"I'm going to have a chat… with my Mum."

"No!" Screamed Jason.

"Zenith, has Ma'am ever referred to me as being her son, in your presence?"

"I'm unable to access that information from my internal memory drive, as there's a firewall in place."

"Oh, is there now? Err, umm… override the firewall."

"Access denied." Replied Zenith.

"Why would she have a firewall installed for such a random question? Zenith, hold the captain here until I return," I said, as I pack my book into my rucksack. "I've got lots of questions that need answering."

"No, you cannot enter… no!" Yelped the struggling Captain.

"Zenith, if he tries to escape, ring his bloody neck."

"Affirmative."

Opening one of the doors, I make my way through to the hallway, that leads to Ma'am's office and proceed into her room, due to the door being left ajar.

"Where is she?" I asked myself as I position the door to the way it was before I entered.

The air conditioning unit in the room blasts-out ice cold air, which is greatly needed, as my face feels like it's about to explode, down to the performance in the Chamber.

I move past her desk sweating, toward another door to the right, which appears to be locked from the inside. On her desk stands an upright picture frame which holds an old, weathered photo of a baby, cuddling a soft plush monkey toy. The toy itself forces me to fall back into her seat, because it's almost like the pieces of this complex puzzle are now falling into place.

Why doesn't she have any photos of my siblings?

"That must have been me when I was a baby." I quietly said to myself, while studying the black and white photo, that shows a blood spot on the toddler's left eye.

The locking mechanism begins to rattle from the inside of the closed door to the right, so I take an enormous deep breath and quietly dart over to the wall. I pin myself tight against the wallpapered wall and watch on as the door slowly opens outwardly, luckily concealing me even more.

"Ma'am, I'll check on Sharpe, he may very well have left. Poor fella, he has been waiting for hours," said Andy, making his way to the door that leads-out to the hall. "If he hasn't, get yourself prepared and contact me once you're ready to see him... I'll talk to him in the meantime."

"I can't let my (one) and only Son go on that treacherous journey," remarked Ma'am from beyond the opened door. "Perhaps I can get him signed-up to join the C-sectors. I spoke to Captain Noolan about it, but he wasn't convinced. Apparently, Paul doesn't like them."

My emotions consume me to the point that I feel like I'm drowning. Why has she kept this hidden from me?

"He's your son... do what you feel is necessary. I did as you asked. I tried to invite him to the gym, but I could tell he's not one bit interested."

Hmm, so that's why Andy was rambling-on about him needing a spotter, and what's all this about trying to sign me up to the C-sectors? I'm not joining those pack of bums.

Andy examines his enormous biceps in the mirror, forcing me to tuck myself behind the opened door even more so, so that he doesn't see me.

"The nurse has left the door open again Ma'am... you need to have a word with her, because I'm sick and tired of having to repeat myself! I'll lock it up."

"Thanks Andy… I'll have a word," Replied Ma'am, from the distance.

The stiff idiot now departs the room, closing and locking the door behind himself.

I slide around the opened door like a baz-rat and swiftly enter the short hallway that leads to the mysterious room. The room itself is larger than her office and is completely white in colour, similar to a room you'd find in a posh hospital. She stands in front of the hospital bed typing on some sort of machine, that appears to be maintaining the oxygen supply to the mysterious patient in the bed.

"He's done what," asked Ma'am, pinching her earlobe with a shaking hand. "He's in my quarters? But how?"

"Mother," I said, watching her slowly turn around to my location.

"No! How did you get in here?"

"Look, just be more open and transparent with me from now on in. I've heard absolutely everything you've said."

An awkward silence hangs over us, as we continue to gaze into each other's eyes.

I immediately target my interest onto the jumpsuit that hangs off a fancy wooden coat rack, to the right, and proceed to break the silence by walking towards her location.

"The lady who visited me when I was in the bunker of Alpha Fifteen, and when I was outside Old Islington Mall... it, it was you," I said, drawing nearer to where she uncomfortably stands. "That's the all-in-one, white jumpsuit... right?"

Another awkward silence emits, forcing her to break her gaze.

"Yes, it was me. Region-Five holds many secret's, secret's that you deserve to know," replied mum, pinching her earlobe. "Andy, tell Zenith that Ma'am orders him to stand down. Keep yourself, the captain, and Zenith outside. I need some private time with my son."

I gulp.

"Son, everything I'm about to say to you is totally down to yourself to either accept... or reject."

"Go ahead then?" I replied, shaking like a leaf.

"Son (Paul) I'm terribly sorry... I had no choice but to give you a way to my sister. That night I handed you over, was extremely hard."

"So, the woman I grew up believing to be my mother, was really my aunt? So that means my siblings are really my cousins? I was told that my father died storming the beaches of south Zakataria... this man was merely my uncle? Why, why did you give me away?"

"Correct. I'm terribly sorry. This wouldn't have been the right place to bring up a child. You required the tender loving care of a family unit, not an artificial home like this. Look around you... underneath these plastered, wallpapered walls is nothing but metal rivets and steel panels. There's no sunlight here, no nothing."

"I'm by no means judging your actions Mother. You didn't deny me the love and affection, believe me. If anything, you was very prudent to be fair. I've only been inside this Ice Wall for a couple of weeks and it's already getting me down. I just can't believe it?"

My mother now takes both of my hands and places my scarred palms against her forehead, "Paul, when I handed you over to my sister, I almost died. It will haunt me until the day I die."

"But why," I asked with tears now rolling down both cheeks. "Why couldn't you just leave the Ice Rim with me?"

"Your father's position within the Zuntran authorities, along with his injuries prohibited him from leaving. He dedicated his entire life to the cause."

"This man in the bed, who's he... is this man my father," I asked, peering around her left shoulder. "What happened to him and why is his face bandaged up like that?"

"Your father was blinded in an assassination attempt, back in Greenshore, many, many years ago. He has remained here ever since, under the full protection of the Southern Alliance and APEX."

"Father," I said working my way around to his bedside. "Can he hear me?"

Mum wipes the flurry of tears away that had built-up under her eyes, "Of course he can. He was up and about, up until he had the devastating stroke."

I study the mysterious man who lays in the bed and spot my soft toy monkey, which looks to have been propped-up beside his head.

My heart beats erratically.

"I remember playing with that specific toy. Mother, is my father aware of my presence?"

"Theodore... your son Paul is here. He has turned out to be a fine young gentleman. He reminds me so much of you."

I recoil from his side and step backwards, "Theodore... Theodore who?"

"Why, Theodore Hammic," replied mum, who now frowns at my startled behaviour. "This was another reason why I couldn't risk you being here. Should anyone (out of my inner circle) have found out, that you're Theodore's, one and only son, it may have very well have attracted some unwanted attention."

I now feel like I'm going to faint from the revelations.

"Paul, you could have been murdered, which is the main reason why we handed you over to my sister. The enemy was hellbent on ending your father's life, hence why we had to fake his burial."

"Are you telling me that my father has been on the Zuntran throne ever since?"

"Yes, to a certain extent."

"What about our current President, Zack Steeling?"

"Zack was drafted in at the time as a ploy, to draw attention away," said Mum, looking at my father. "Although, your father still has his overall say in matters. I'm merely his conduit and spokesperson."

Confused I ask, "How is he communicative?"

"Your Father communicates using his left hand. He can write so beautifully, when he has enough energy, although he's been extremely weak, as of late."

"So, he can hear me," I asked, grabbing hold of his left-hand. "Father, how are you? Err, sorry, I know it's a bit foolish of me to ask. Hmm, it's your son (Paul)."

"Yes, he can hear absolutely everything."

My Father tenses-up with a tight grip and doesn't let go.

This was obviously the man whom I had seen during my near-death experience. The one where the mysterious man lifted me up from out of my cot. Damn, I'm the son of President Hammic... that's crazy.

"The toy monkey? I remember playing with it in my soft-meshed cot, when I was a baby," I sobbingly said. "Sorry, I'm just trying to process everything."

A tear escapes from under my father's bandage and slowly rolls down to his right ear.

Mum cries also and then begins to battle the tears by saying, "Right-right, I must get back to my duties."

"I understand," I said, wiping away the tears with my free hand. "But you still haven't explained to me, how you visited me inside Alpha Fifteen's bunker, and outside Old Islington Mall?"

"We call it the (all seeing eye) or (eye) for short. It's been a classified top secret. We first stumbled across the weapon when the Alliance first infiltrated this Ice Region, well before the (Hero) mission."

"So, the Zuntran authorities knew the earth was flat way before the mission?"

"Yes… but we needed to provide more credible evidence to the masses, hence why we initiated (Hero). Alan Watt and those alike weren't enough to wake-up the people of the disc."

"Interesting… can you please continue about the (eye) Mother?"

"We now know (with the help of our scientists and researchers) that the pyramid structure was used as a tool/weapon by the Watchers, to install fear into the minds of the entire population."

"But why," I intriguingly asked. "And who are the Watchers?"

"To reinforce certain core belief systems. The Watchers used it to scare folk into believing their narratives. They would present themselves as gods to those whom they would target (like I did with you) making the observer think they were being contacted by a higher divine force. Little did the observers know, they were really being watched/visited by the angelic mafia."

"But who are they? Are they upgraded Spectres?"

"No, they look exactly like us. They are multi-generational, highly intelligent humans, who've have been orchestrating everything inside the Dome (with the help of the Spectres) since the dawn of mankind."

"It's all starting to make perfect sense now. So, they the Watchers, basically brainwashed people with counterfeit visions, to help bolster the people's belief in Zeno, the god of the Zunnha religion, so they could extract valuable resources from them and follow their narratives?"

"Precisely. They also used the (eye) to haunt people, like paranormal activity, ghosts, sleep paralyses etc, and also utilised it to promote the expansive universe, by dressing up as Aliens. We've even got their grey, zip-up costumes, that they the (watchers) wore to traumatise people."

"Damn. Where is the (eye) and how big is it?"

"It's currently guarded in between this level and the lower level. It looks like a giant four-sided pyramid, that you enter into from a doorway at the bottom. Once comfortably seated inside, it allows the user to leave their body, to freely travel around the disc."

"That's crazy," I replied. "How does it feel to be outside of one's body?"

"Hmm, it's very similar to having a lucid dream. It's like your spirit is being freed from your body. The structure itself is totally made out of gold/silver and various other unknown metals. I'd say, the structure is about, eight metres in height, from its base to its apex."

"Really?"

"Yes. It was heavily guarded by the enemy when we first infiltrated the Ice Rim, but we managed to successfully flush them out."

"That's incredible. I had a premonition about the hypersonic missile strikes... did the (all seeing eye) have anything to do with that experience?"

"It was me. I tried to warn you. Obviously, I didn't mean to scare you. I literally entered the threat into your dreamworld, by focusing-in on the risks, using my own thoughts. I'm sorry if it impacted you in such an upsetting way. I'm the only person trained to use it."

"Wow, I knew that there was something in that strange message."

"Please forgive me... I knew it would frighten you, but I needed to warn you... they could have attacked your location at any given moment."

"I hold zero animosity to your overall decision-making Mother. It sounds like you've been through hell and back."

Mum cries.

"I need to know everything about the Spectres and Watchers... can you enlighten me some more?"

"Paul, what do you already know?"

"Captain Noolan said that the (Spectre) are the caretakers of this dome, however he's unsure of their true origin. He hasn't indulged into the Watchers? I knew nothing about their existence up until now? Honest."

"Captain Noolan, is right about the Spectre... I can confirm this empirically. The Spectre were specifically used by the Watchers as their very own worker bees, within this (hive) Ice Wall. The captain knows all about the Watchers, but has been briefed not to disclose such information, as their existence is highly restricted."

"But why is the Watchers existence being kept so hush-hush?"

"We've kept the news of the Watchers classified, down to the simple fact of (not) wanting to drop such immeasurable information onto the laps of those who are already grappling with the magnitude of us living under a dome. One must realise that these facets of data need to be presented in stages, to avoid all out chaos."

"But why? The truth is the truth?"

"Okay, let me give you an example. Err, imagine if you lived in Zakataria, or its neighbouring Allied territories, and you believed wholeheartedly in the spherical globe earth model, along with the Zunnha God (Zeno) all in which have been brought on by years and years of indoctrination.

"Right," I replied with an intrigued head on. "I guess my mind would be cemented into believing just that, especially if those around me are also brainwashed."

"Exactly. There would be no point of us disclosing such information of the Watcher's existence, further afield, because it wouldn't register with your worldview anyway, and I guess it would come across as, perhaps too far-fetched, particularly if you've dismissed the elephant in the room beforehand, being the factual (Flat Earth) evidence."

"Yeah, but I'm not talking about revealing it to the Zakatarians or its axis of pure unadulterated evil. I'm talking about Zuntra and its Allied nations? Why haven't our very own people been told?

"Our people and our Allies are already up against it, both in the Rim and on the terrain. We've had families displaced by the perpetual conflict, which has caused immense heartache and pain. The Southern Alliance is committed to capturing the entire rim, which will subsequently allow us to implement our own world order. Once we have done so, then we will be in the position to elaborate on our findings, and hopefully bring those responsible to justice. Our main target now is to destroy the Spectres. Once we've done that, then we can bring the Watchers to justice."

"Hmm, right okay."

"The Spectre's main duties (before we infiltrated the Ice Rim) comprised of many operational tasks. The Watchers would use them to transport themselves to and from Region-Five and would also task them with the movement of the valuable resources, via the tunnels that link each of the Regions. However, we appear to have stirred-up their hive, hence why the Spectres now have an obvious presence."

"Interesting." I replied.

"They, the Watchers, use the people of the disc to extract valuable materials from under the terrain/surface, which they then get the Spectre to store inside Region-Twelve. Our military hasn't reached that far yet, but our scouts have. They apparently control all four domes, well, let me rephrase that a bit better, because we are in the process of eliminating them, in this specific dome."

"Fascinating. So, Scott, and Mr Watt was right after all."

"Scott? Oh, your friend, the one you managed to save in Zakataria. I've got to say, your heroics haven't gone unnoticed Son."

"Yeah, I thought he was a tinfoil hat nut job. Turns out I was wrong, although Scott and Alan, did say that they, the Spectres were Aliens."

"The absolute origin of the Spectres is still unknown, so I wouldn't want to surmise just yet, on that particular subject. Although, going on the evidence we have, it does suggest a higher intelligence controls them... whom we believe to be the Watchers."

"I take it you're holding the Watchers here as prisoners?"

"No, the ones we captured inside the Ice Wall, all committed suicide, using suicide pills. Thirty-three of them were taken-in as prisoners, by the Southern Alliance and simultaneously killed themselves-off, using pills hidden away in their capped-molars."

"Wow."

"Extensive research has revealed that the (Watchers) were placed into their positions, both here at the Ice wall and Zakataria, to manage the dome, using the Spectre and Zakatarians as their henchmen. The Spectre were originally only localised to the Ice Wall, yet down to our gradual superiority, they've been scattered all around the disc, to help aid a revival."

"But who put the Watchers at the top of the food chain?"

"That's the age-old question? Adjacent to the (eye) is the Dome's main control centre. There's one control centre and (eye) to each Rim."

"So, each Dome have these situated in their Rims?"

"Yes. The large mysterious Chamber is where the Watchers orchestrated everything, from tsunamis, floods and asteroids. It was also used as a means to contact the Watchers of the adjoining Domes too."

"How did they create asteroids, floods etc? And what happened to the communication link with the Watchers inside the neighbouring Domes?"

"Pyrotechnics. The asteroids are literally like a firework display, in the crudest way possible. The large boiling rocks are exploded-out from the Ice Rim and can travel for thousands of miles, giving the obvious effect of an asteroid/comet. Floods and tsunamis are also created by the Rim, via the main control centre. We literally have the power to flood the entire Dome, at the push of a button, hence why we've secured its location. This is made possible by the inlet and outlet valves, that surround the bottom parts of the circular Ice Wall."

"Wow. That's absolutely mad."

"I know son. As for the Watchers, we've been camouflaging ourselves as the Watchers of Zeno-Three, in the hope that it doesn't alarm those in the neighbouring domes… and to a certain degree it has worked, because we only send them updates via written messages. God forbid what would happen if they sussed us out."

"What would happen mother?"

"They could very well send in the cavalry."

"Hmm. Let's hope that doesn't happen then. Mum… or Mother, I've got one last question, that I really need you to answer?"

"Go ahead Son?"

"My application to join the Aurora… will you allow me to go?"

My father tightens his grasp even more so, and then presses it down into his mattress.

"Mother, what's he doing? What is he trying to say?"

"He's signalling to us both that he wants you to go and explore beyond our dome, my dear," said mum, as she expels yet more tears from her big brown bloodshot eyes. "And I'm not going to be the one to stand in the way of your wishes."

The monitor starts to bleep erratically as I wipe away my tears.

"No! He's having another heart attack… hurry we've got to help him," Screamed my mother, pressing down on her earlobe.

"No… no way!" I cried clutching his hand.

"Andy… get help. Hurry, its Theodore! I think he's having another episode."

Operation Optima

I lay on my bed with a slight headache brought on by the shenanigans of last night's drinking session. Harnessing the pulsating pain, by using my fingertips, I gently push on both throbbing temples.

"Damn, I better get my arse into gear," I said to myself, as I squint at the clock that is stood on my bedside cabinet. "Hmm, Captain Noolan will be here for me soon."

I rollover on my side and stretch-out my body, which instantly creates a creaking sound, followed by a crunching crack in my lower-back and ankles.

"Fud it. I shouldn't have been so greedy with all that booze."

Rolling onto my back, I now stare at the ceiling's silver riveted panels and begin to think back about yesterday. The day started off with a bang (metaphorically speaking).

Captain Noolan was banging down the door of my quarters; his boisterous behaviour when I answered the door was somewhat startling, because I'd never witnessed him being so overly chuffed with himself before... well, not like that anyway.

He instantly grabbed hold of my elbows and shook them with pure delight. Entering my room, he reached over to the sound system and clicked its power switch. The random music bellowed out of the room, forcing me to slam the door shut, to which I was then forcefully made to participate in his moronic dancing routine, until I was totally spent. I'll openly admit it, I can't dance for toffee.

Having exhausted himself to the point of no return, he then turned the volume down and proceeded to let me in on the gossip, by throwing himself backwards onto my bed. He told me that we had been given clearance by the engineers, whom had been working night and day on the Aurora's upgrades and said that we were to link-up with both Alex Pale and Mr Watt etc, for a farewell celebratory drink, which had been organised by my mother; although down to the death of my father, she sadly refrained from joining us.

My father (Theodore Hammic) unfortunately passed away a few hours after I had brazenly entered into his room. I really don't think the news has sunk-in yet, and I'm still unsure what to make of it all. The whole revelation thing was truly upsetting, to be brutally honest, but I somehow weathered the emotional storm, with the helping hand of Racheal (the medic who had gifted me the journal prior).

Racheal and her colleagues raced into the room and immediately went to work on stabilising my father's breathing, however after a heart wrenching emotional plea from my mother, to end his suffering, with various drugs etc, he let go of his life, whilst still holding my clammy hand.

It was so surreal, watching them all running around the room in a panic and to a certain degree, it really did put it all into perspective for me, in regard to how important he was to the Southern Alliance.

After he died my mum was constantly inundated with messages of condolence, from all Allied

Presidents/Representatives etc. Her phone didn't stop ringing.

They (the medical staff) all worked tremendously hard to preserve his life, but in the bitter end, there was absolutely nothing else they could possibly do for him. I suppose, it is what it is.

Looking back at it, it was almost like he was hanging-on in there, just to meet me, in a strange sort of way... pretty much like destiny/karma.

It's been five days now since that chaotic event and I'm still trying to get my head around it all. I guess if it hadn't of been for the captain slipping-up in the Chamber, I'd have been none the wiser, which just goes to show that when something doesn't ring right, one must press-on, by grabbing the bull by its fudding horns. Look at it this way... if I hadn't of been so adamant, I'd be still living in the dark.

Racheal (the medic) held back with me while my mother was preparing to move his body to the highly secretive, Middle-Level, the one which holds the (eye) and the main control centre of the dome. Apparently, they (my mother and the authorities) are planning to have his ashes scattered across Greenshore, as it seems it's what he had wished for prior. From what I've heard, they'll achieve this by releasing the ashes from a Zuntran screamer plane.

So yeah, where was I?

Oh, that's it. Racheal and I spoke for hours afterwards, although I had to play dumb. My mother had pulled me to one side during the failed resuscitation of my father, warning me not to share my connection of being his one and only son, although standing there holding his hand, crying, did raise a few eyebrows, I must say.

Racheal and I eventually made it out of my mother's quarters, to the sound of distant thunder, and quietly entered into the observation room, which is adjacent to the Chamber, to view the Zuntran Ocean from its reinforced window; the violent flurry of raindrops hitting the Rim from the storm outside was absolutely pummelling the large oval shaped window and sounded very melodic.

It was there where we spontaneously kissed each other, under both the light of the artificial moon, and the uninvited thunder strikes. The sinister bolts of lightning forced us ever so closer, until we were glued together. Her breasts squeezed against my stomach as she drew me in with a tight hug. After the heart pounding exchange of intimacy, we then cozied-up on the sofa and entwined. I was scared because I've never had anyone touch me in that way before.

Racheal spoke of her life before moving to the Rim, by sharing her past and present experiences, which were awfully similar to mine in a strange kind of way. She had unfortunately lost both parents during the onslaught of the Zakatarian invasion, the one that occurred on the first anniversary of the (Hero Mission). She didn't stop crying in my arms.

It was awfully hard controlling my emotions, because all I kept thinking about was my aunt, the one whom I'd grow-up believing to be my mother.

After a timely duration of back-and-forth questioning, we both parted ways, down to Captain Noolan, who rudely stumbled in on us.

So yeah, I suppose I've now got myself a friend here, which has already started to wreak havoc with my already erratic emotions, because I don't really want to part ways from her. But hey, it's a little bit late now, seeing that my journal is now the key to the mission.

Last night's drinking session started in the Chamber and was then moved to the observation room, due to the long and anticipated, Grayson Furious vs Chiroza fight. Big bald Grayson (the furious one) won by unanimous decision and left the Chamber to celebrate in the lower level, with his entourage of diehard fans, along with the crew of the (Sapphire) who were also present for the first mission briefing.

I spoke to Josh, Jhita and Yogi for a short time before the initial rundown of the mission. They were still pretty cut-up about Hersh, especially Josh, seeing that he had known him well before us. To be honest, nobody really delved too much into the subject, probably down to the devastating circumstances surrounding it all, I guess. Hersh truly was Araqia's finest, no doubt about it.

We, Captain Noolan and I held back in the Observation room, with both Alex Pale and Alan Watt, to discuss the objectives of the mission a little further, which has been officially code-named, Operation Optima.

Both Watt, Pale and Jinta had originally wrote up a plan of action, that would see us contacting a target in Zeno Four, who is known to be an artist by the name of David Hammond. Apparently, this David guy is one of a very few within Zeno Four, who's open to the possibility that they could be living under a dome. According to both Watt and Pale etc, his artwork and social media accounts are what is needed to promote the truth to the masses, as he could draw-in an influential following.

The crew of the pantheon, who are located inside a cave below Zeno Four's Region Five, had sent all of this mysterious chap's social media posts, uploads, messages and video uploads over to the Southern Alliance.

They, both the Southern Alliance and APEX have decided that if they can create a vessel of communication with this guy, we may be able to use his artwork etc, as a way of breaking the population of Zeno Four's paradigm shackles. The majority of the folk under that specific dome are said to be suffering from extreme cognitive dissonance.

Having heard our objectives of locating the person of interest, I immediately stood up at the table and began to rummage through my rucksack.

The conversation between us all, went something like this:

"Wait!" I exclaimed, looking at the group of individuals who were necking their stimulants.

"What's up?" Replied the Captain.

Everyone at the table paused in sheer suspense as they eagerly waited for what I had to offer them.

I grabbed hold of my journal and slid it across the large round table to Alex Pale, who was scratching at his crown, totally perplexed.

Having now got their full attention I then proceeded to offer them another angle.

"We need to think outside of the box. Everything I've experienced in my life is written down in that book, along with the current situation we are now finding ourselves in. We obviously cannot go in there with all gun's blazing, so the only other way around it is to create material, using the arts, literature etc, to slowly wake them up, without the need of bloodshed... a bloodless war, so to speak."

"Hmm... I'm interested." Said Alex pale, signalling to the bartender for a top-up.

"We obviously can't just rock up in there and drop the information on their laps. It has to be a slow process. Combining the book with his artwork will most certainly speed things up, in regard to waking them up from their coma."

Everyone at the table looked at each other, in an intrigued manner.

"Continue?" Asked Alex Pale.

I went on to say, "If this David guy could incorporate his artwork inside my story, it would increase our chances of reversing the conditioning, far more efficiently."

"Coupling both forms of art would subsequently accelerate our agenda further," said Watt, removing his fedora to wipe the beads of sweat from his forehead. "If this guy (David) was able to get it published, it would create a tsunami of consciousness to ripple throughout their dome, and ultimately break down the doors in which they have unknowingly been imprisoned behind. It'll crack the dome, metaphorically speaking. Oh, and they share the same language as us... it's a brilliant idea."

The table fell silent until Alex Pale raised his glass of fine Carrikian whisky into the air to say, "I see you've got a chapter called, Flat Earth... I think this is truly an excellent idea. The possibilities are endless. Should we pull this off, it'll be truly extraordinary. The people within that Dome deserve to know the truth... and if we can do it in such a covert manner, that'll not cause suspicion, it will no doubt cause that rippling wave we so badly desire... Sharpe, your journal will be the key to success here. I'm in favour. Buy the way, I see you've called your story Greenshore... hmm, nice touch.

"But what happens afterwards?"

Alan Watt readjusts his fedora and replies, "Captain Noolan, haven't you been listening? If this is pulled-off, we could establish ourselves there far quicker, and have the backing of their people in a shorter timeframe. An illustrative novel/book promoting the Domes could create an enormous following... a following that we will most certainly need, should we introduce/establish ourselves there. When the book hits the shelves, we will plan for our APEX personnel to infiltrate their rim. We can create various movements to protest against the Watchers and their (lap dog) Spectres. The vast majority of people inside that dome are deeply asleep sheep. They still think they're spinning around on a ball, at one thousand miles per hour, for crying out loud."

The whole table erupted with laughter.

"No... I was merely inquiring about what we are to do after we complete the transfer of Sharpe's journal etc, to this David Hammond guy... and anyway, what if this chap refuses to work with us?"

"Oh, I see. I do apologise. If he refuses to work with you Captain... I want you to transport him to the outside of his Dome, so he can see the darn thing for himself. From our in-depth investigation of the fine gentleman, he'll bite your hands off anyway. His social media is constantly inundated with Flat Earth material, conspiracy, cover-ups, etc. He is our guy. Once you've briefed him and handed him Sharpe's journal, yourself Sharpe, Hughes and Zenith are to go forth to Zeno One and establish a communication outpost there, similar to what the crew of Pantheon have achieved in Zeno Four. Please, when you arrive to the cave, make sure you connect to Pantheon's communication transmitter, so Captain Lex, can transfer your data to us. You're to remain hidden until told otherwise."

The captain nodded his head in agreement and asked, "Mr Pale. What about Sapphire and its crew... when will they be arriving to Zeno Four?"

"I've already briefed them earlier on. They will arrive to Zeno Four with supplies for the Pantheon crew. Should you encounter any problems, you're to call upon them for assistance. Once you've departed, Sapphire will covertly move-in and protect the target, because you'll need to scan the surface area on the way to Zeno One. When that book gains momentum, the watchers may very well want to terminate David Hammond, black-ops assassination style. We'll be briefing them again anyway."

"Right, got you… I just wanted to clear that up."

"No… that's perfectly fine Captain," said Alex Pale. "I'm glad you're asking questions. On your arrival to Zeno-Four, I want you to liaise with the crew of the Pantheon, before you proceed to David Hammond. Just make sure you make them aware of your presence and obviously send us your scans, images etc, of the dome and surface area."

"Affirmative."

"That folder in front of you Captain Noolan, contains everything you need to know about our man of interest, along with the location of where he resides. We've been tracking his routes to and from work and have also amassed lots of information of the particular places he visits. The safest place to introduce yourselves to him would be on his way to work. He travels along a rather long dirt road that is completely surrounded by greenery. It's imperative you keep a low profile. You'll need to use your own initiative to get his attention. I believe there's a derelict farm nearby, perhaps you could launch the mission from there?"

"Interesting." Replied the Captain.

"We even know this guy's hobbies, likes/dislikes etc. Everything is written down in that folder. By the way, you'll need to be extremely cautious in London city."

"Why?" asked the captain.

"London, the city in which David Hammond resides within, is plagued with gang warfare, although the weapons you have at your disposal are far more superior to theirs... so please, just be vigilant."

The captain immediately stood up from his seat, "Gangs... what sort of gangs?"

A pang of fear uninvitingly erupted in my stomach, forcing me to tense up my six-pack. My meeting with the Teddy Boys back at Old Crusty's Diner was looming over my shoulders like a devilish shadow. Just the thought of a skirmish with an unknown gang of individuals was enough to make me want to remain in the Rim for eternity.

"Like I've already said… everything you'll need is inside that folder. Please make sure you read every paragraph thoroughly."

"Bang" "Bang" "Bang"

The large thunderous bangs to my door force me to jolt in my bed.

"Captain, is that you?"

"Yes… Sharpe, pack that journal away now. We need to get going."

"Wait, for crying out loud," I yelled, while observing my missing left eyebrow in the mirror. "Some mother fudder has removed my eyebrow… bazturds."

Having cleaned myself up I finally zip-up my armoured vest and take a deep breath.

Farewell Thief

"Sharpe, come on we must go," said the captain thumping my door again.

"Wait, for crying out loud!" I yelled while observing my missing left eyebrow once more.

"Bang" "Bang" Bang"

"I'm coming, I'm coming... stop banging my fudding door down." I stammered.

I tie-up my boot laces and then retrieve my rucksack from my bed. Turning the locking mechanism of the doorknob to the left, I depart my quarters.

"Look, some fudder has cut off my eyebrow."

The captain chuckles, "Serves you right... you was absolutely wasted last night. Big Andy had to carry you here."

"Damn, how embarrassing. I could murder a hot cup of latte. Can we stop to get one?"

"We must hurry Sharpe. Hughes has injured his knee to the extent that he will not be able to join us for the objectives. Sharpe, we need someone to take his place, otherwise they may postpone the mission altogether... I was thinking about offering it to Watson, but I'm not sure?"

"See, I told you... Hughes is nothing but a knucklehead. I knew he'd injure himself. Backflips/handstands, the guy is a fudding lunatic. Watson is another one. He was probably responsible for my missing eyebrow actually. The immature fudder."

"What do you suggest then?" Asked the Captain, as we make our way down the hall, just passed the Chambers entrance.

"I suggest we bring Scott on board."

"Yes, but you said his knees are knackered. We can't afford to take anyone with injuries buddy."

"He'll be good to go Captain. He has been having various injections for his kneecaps. Trust me, he's the one."

"Okay… but we don't have the time to fud around here for caffe latte. We need to collect him now and leave immediately. Is he still on that military ward?"

"No, I spoke to him on the phone yesterday morning. The medical staff moved him into the main civilian ward, as the military section is absolutely rammed with casualties."

The captain presses his earlobe, "Ma'am, do you copy over?"

"Please ask her to inform Racheal of our departure." I asked.

"Most certainly, Sharpe." Replied the captain.

"I'm great Ma'am… can you please inform Mr Pale that we have a substitute for Hughes… Private, Luke Scott, has been highly recommended by your son," said the captain, turning to look at me. "Sorry, but could you also inform Racheal that Paul will be in the cargo hold in the next half hour. Thanks Ma'am. "

"Right, let's get him," said the captain, pressing on his earlobe once more. "Zenith, do you copy over? Zenith, we're heading down to collect Luke Scott from the hospital ward, on the lower level. Make sure you check over our supplies. Once you've done that, fire-up the engines and check the operating systems. We will be with you shortly."

"Is the Aurora ready for action?"

"Yes Sharpe. The upgrades are complete. Listen," said the captain looking over his right shoulder. "I'm so sorry about your father passing away."

"Thanks. It's fine. I didn't really know the man. I'm still trying to wrap my head around it, to be fair. It's been very hard."

"Would you like to see your mother before we head-off?"

"No… she's in a bad way and I don't really want to add to it," I replied passing the main chamber. "She might try and throw a spanner in the works."

"I know, I know. Hear me out… you'll need to keep the knowledge of your parents undisclosed to absolutely everyone… that applies to Scott also."

"I understand Captain. I've been briefed by my mother already."

"I'm so glad that I slipped up about Ma'am being your mother, although I nearly krud my pants when you set Zenith against me. He could have popped my head like a grape."

I instantly chuckle, "Yeah, sorry about that, but it's a good job I did, otherwise I'd have been none the wiser. And to top that off… I could have been Andy's spotter."

"You don't like Andy, do you?"

"I don't mind him... he's just a bit of a knucklehead." I replied.

"It was extremely hard holding all that information against you Sharpe. Knowing that secret since you was a child, was absolute torture, especially not that long ago, when you mentioned about the documentary (Zuntra and its struggle). I just couldn't enter into any kind of dialogue with you about it, down to the fact that I knew President Hammic was your father."

"I thought it was a bit odd, when you said you wasn't interested in history or politics Captain?"

"I was merely diverting you away from the topic/subject of your father, just in case I may have slipped-up. Sharpe, I really am my own worst enemy at times."

"Hmm, like I said, it sounded really strange... especially coming from such an inquisitive person like yourself."

"Captain," said Stuart behind his desk. "Paul Sharpe, how are you both?"

"Great, and yourself?" I replied.

"Splendid," Replied Stuart. "I take it you are both here for your pistols."

"Indeed, we are. Stuart, I do hope all is well. How's the family?"

"They are on route to this Region as we speak Captain. Apparently, they're being escorted by the Phoenix."

"Sharpe's brother serves on board that mighty vessel... your family is in safe hands I can assure you."

"Really... that's good to know," replied Stuart collecting our pistols from their designated lockers. "Here you go guys. Captain... once again, thank you ever so much for all you have done for us."

"No, the pleasure is all mine. Just make sure to tell them I said hello, and that they are most welcome. Sharpe and I here need to press-on, hopefully we will see you on our return."

"Take good care the pair of you... stay strong and safe."

We depart Stuart's location and head toward the lift shaft to the right of the hallway.

"Sharpe, I know Thomas isn't your real brother, but we must stick to the story."

"That's fine... honestly, I understand. So, Captain, what's the plan?"

"We collect Scott and head-off into the sunset," replied the captain, hitting the switch for the lift. "How's your head?"

"Perhaps I shouldn't have been so greedy with all that stout. I'm okay though. You did very well by not indulging in the drink... I'm extremely proud of you."

"Got to keep a clean head-on. How many pints did you end up having?" Asked the Captain.

"Four."

"You're a lightweight."

"I know, I know." I replied deflated.

The elevator swiftly arrives. We both enter into the lift, which is totally packed-out with two groups of C-sectors. One of the group are the ones whom we encountered at the upper-level cargo hold, before we departed for (Operation Deep Freeze).

"Gentlemen." Said the Captain with a cheeky smirk.

The C-sectors totally ignore the captain's welcome and carry on conversing with each other about their experiences with the large civilian population, of the lower level, along with updates about a suspected thief, who's apparently robbing from the people below.

"Hey, it's those two," remarked one of the kruds. "You know, the ones who tried to evade us. He's only got one eyebrow?"

"Oh, you're right," said the overzealous one chuckling to his colleague. "Can we browse your identification cards... do you get it lads...(brows) your identification cards?"

The three idiots, along with the other group of C-sectors laugh ever so loudly, making the lift rattle and shake.

The captain immediately turns around, "Look... don't let the power go to your head son. You are merely a servant to those who reside in this Rim. Should you wish to continue your tyrannical pursuit, you'll leave me with no other option but to have your uniform/badge removed. I'm not playing around."

"Who do you think you are?"

"I'm Captain Jason Noolan of the Aurora, APEX personnel, number, two nine, eight seven... now should you wish to continue talking like we can't hear you; you'll leave me with no other option but to inform your higher ranking official (chief Monroe) at the upper-level C-section."

"You know Monroe? I'm, terribly sorry Captain," replied the cowardly C-sector, now lowering his head in shame. "I do apologise."

"Apology accepted. Have a pleasant day… oh and make sure you find that thief," said the captain, returning to admire himself in the reflective glass doors of the lift.

After a long awkward descent, the doors finally open up to the chaotic scenes of the overpopulated lower-level section. Large groups of people bundle together for warmth by huddling around large radiator pipes. The persistent sound of crying babies and people conversing totally wreaks my already pounding head, obviously brought on by my hangover and the nonsense inside the lift.

"Fud, this place is absolutely mad," I said observing the large, reinforced gates, that separate the people from gaining access to the upper level. "We need to go through that middle archway, I think?"

"Right, where's the hospital." Asked the Captain showing the C-sectors at the checkpoint his APEX identification.

"Civilian or military?" Asked the C-sector

"Err, where did you say he was Sharpe?"

"He's been moved to the civilian section. It's through that archway." I replied.

"You'll need to go through the archway directly in front of you. Follow it all the way to the end, and you'll come to the adult ward entrance. It's extremely busy."

"See, I told you it's through there."

"Sorry, I obviously didn't hear you Sharpe."

We depart the control desk and walk through the electronic gates. Stepping over toys and other obstacles left in the way by the playing children, we head for the archway and continue down the tunnel.

Both sides of the cramped tunnel are rammed packed with families who are using the tunnel as their new home. They awkwardly stare at us as we pass them, in our black uniforms and side arms.

"I can't believe how busy it is down here."

"I know Sharpe, I can't even think with all this bloody noise going on."

We now make it out of the freezing cold tunnel and into a large hall, similar to the Chamber.

"Fud it's freezing down here. That's the entrance over there."

"Are you sure, Sharpe?"

"Positive. Look, it states it on the sign above."

"Great," replied the captain. "What makes you think that he'll accept the offer of joining us. We could very well be wasting our time down here."

"Trust me… he'll bite your hands off," I said, nearing to the desk which has twenty-or-so people queueing-up. "Scott would literally die to be given the opportunity… trust me."

"We'll have to disclose the offer to him once we are clear from here though. This information is strictly confidential to only those of us in the know."

"Affirmative Captain. I'll keep it on the low."

A strange looking elderly chap screams obscenities at the lady behind the desk. The man is very well dressed considering, and his shoes look immaculately clean.

My mum... oops, I mean my aunt would always tell me to be very wary of people with extremely clean shoes... she was a very superstitious lady.

"I demand you to let me through, now! I've got to collect some medication, otherwise I may collapse... and if I do, I'll make sure you're both held responsible... you silly looking women. Why are you not listening to me?" asked the disgruntled man to the seated lady, who's sat behind the left side of the reception desk.

"This is going to be fun," said the captain, looking through the window of the door that leads to the various wards.

"Hi. How can I help you both?"

"Hello, err… both myself and my colleague here need to visit a patient. We are from the upper level."

"What's his, or her name?" Asked the lady seated at the right side of the desk, who calmly sits typing.

The captain fails to reply and immediately turns his interest onto the side profile of the belligerent man.

"You are a stupid, pathetic woman. Look at these two… look everyone. Look, we now have people jumping the fudding queue." Said the rude man to the people queuing up behind him.

The lady on the left instantly asks, "Sir, can you not use such vile language… please?"

"I'll say what I like." Replied the man, staring at us both.

"Ignore him. What's the name of the patient you're here for?"

"Private, Luke Scott." I replied to the lady who is now typing on her mobile phone.

"Oh, the military man?"

"That's correct." I replied.

"Go through the main door and do your first right... he'll be in the ward at the very end. It's called the nightingale ward."

"Great... come on Captain."

The captain tugs onto my left arm, "No... hold on a minute."

"Captain, what's up?"

"This piece of krud needs telling."

"Leave him alone. He's an old man... come on."

"No Sharpe. Err, excuse me sir, but you can't talk to people like this."

"Go away. I'm not talking to you, am I? I'm talking to this useless bitch."

"Right, that's enough!" Exclaimed the Captain.

The old man turns his interest to where we stand and immediately squares-up to the captain, "Keep your nose out of my business, before I bust your face-in. You don't scare me. If you think I'm scared of your uniform, your totally wrong. Look at you both… waltzing around imitating the C-sectors. You and your red eyed friend with the missing eyebrow, can go and do one."

"Leave him be, Captain… he isn't worth it. He's an idiot."

"Surinder Pal," remarked the captain. "You worked in the newsagents that was located in the Red Zone's Islington side."

"Oh fud," I said looking away in sheer fright and disbelief.

"Yes… but I don't know who you are? Look, this silly looking prat of a woman is jeopardising my health, by ignoring my wishes. All I want to do is wait inside where it's warmer and collect my prescription. I've been waiting in the cold for over one hour now."

"I've told the gentleman a number of times already sir, that women and children are to be prioritised over everyone else." Said the lady at the desk.

Surinder Pal bangs his fist down heavily onto the reception desk and yells, "Listen to me, you slag of a woman..."

Without warning the captain grabs hold of Surinder Pal's rather large right ear and twists it, sending an almighty scream to emit from the belligerent mother-fudder's mouth. The echo immediately emits throughout the large Chamber, forcing people to turn around to our location, in fright.

"Now, you better listen to me," exclaimed the captain, drawing him in by the ear. "You don't remember me? Are you sure?"

"Argh! let go of me at once!"

"Remember the young man with the winning lottery ticket? Come on... think back!"

The captain tries to hold back his anger but fails abysmally.

"It's, it's you... no." Stuttered Surinder.

"You denied my mother of medication. You denied my mother of the care she so rightly deserved. You denied me of my winnings. You're nothing but an envious, cancerous, demonic bazturd. You cut my mum's life short. You swine."

"Help!" Yelped Surinder.

"Captain, you're going to end up ripping his ear clean off. It's bleeding."

"Sharpe, shut up... shut the fud up!" Screamed the Captain.

The captain now looks like a man possessed, as he twists Surinder's ear anticlockwise.

"Please-please… I'm sorry-I'm sorry, I remember."

The long line of people now smoulder Surinder Pal with looks that could kill.

"Right, what's going on here," asked a familiar voice coming out from the door, that leads to the ward. "Well, roll-on, Sharpe, what the hell are you doing down here?"

Mickey McNally greets me with a tight squeeze and then instantly peels himself away to sort out the abusive Surinder Pal, whose right ear looks like it's now hanging off.

"Susan… is this the man you messaged me about," asked Mickey. "Jason, how the fud are you fella? Listen-up, I'll take it from here guys."

"Yes Mickey," replied Susan. "That's the man… he was talking when he should have been listening. This gentleman here was only doing what was right."

"That's fine… I know these two fine gentlemen very well. They're my good old friends from the Red Zone."

Mickey pulls the captain away from Surinder, causing blood to trickle out from the fudder's now flapping ear.

"You're bazturds… the lot of you," yelled Surinder, kicking and punching. "I'll report you to the C-sectors."

"Don't you dare talk to our staff in that kind of manner, ever again." Said Mickey, kissing Surinder with one enormous uppercut to the chin.

Surinder gets lifted clean off his feet from the devastating punch and lands heavily on the cold deck in a heap. Gold rings and various other valuables now scatter across the floor, from being ejected out from his inside pockets.

"Oh, my good grief," cried Susan. "Can everyone in the queue please stand back."

She repeats her orders three of four times as the people reluctantly shuffle backwards.

"Oh, it looks like we may have our thief… this krud has been loitering around the wards for days now. Many sleeping patients have had their jewellery pulled from their ears and fingers by this bazturd. He apparently targets the vulnerable. Susan, call for the C-sectors... believe me now, if anyone else here disrespects these fine women, you'll all be getting the same treatment," said Mickey, putting Surinder's lifeless body into the recovery position. "Jason, Sharpe, what brings the pair of you down here... I thought you were both in the military? What are you doing in those uniforms?"

The people in the queue now quietly converse with each other while admiring Mickey's handy-work and the scattered jewellery.

"We are here to collect someone. Our presence here is strictly classified... I'm sorry Mickey, but we are forbidden to indulge."

"Well, roll-on. Okay Jason. Oh, you must be here for the military man then... Luke Scott?"

"That's him."

"He's not that long ago arrived from the military ward though... he's down that hall."

"We know, the helpful lady told us already. Look, we are extremely busy Mickey. We must dash."

"Fine Sharpe... I'll clean up this mess," said Mickey. "Sure, hopefully we can link up for a bite to eat and a few pints... hey guys? "

"We would love to, but we are on a very important mission, so we must dash."

"Get going then," said Mickey. "Susan, call for a stretcher. This fudder is out cold... and come help me collect the evidence."

We depart Mick and enter into the opened door. Turning right we aim our interest to the signs for the nightingale ward.

"Fancy that? First Surinder, then Mickey. It sure is a small dome," I said as we aim for the ward. "Are you alright Captain... you look like you've seen a ghost?"

"Well, I have... a ghost of the past. I'm a little shaken, but I'll be fine Sharpe. Look, I'm sorry for shouting at you back there... it's totally out of character for me to behave in that manner, but I could literally feel the anger changing me inside."

"It's natural… the krud did you dirty. The amount of jewellery he had on his person was absolutely ridiculous. The little no-good crook."

"So, do you believe me about the lottery ticket Sharpe?"

"Come on Captain… I knew you wasn't talking krud back in Zakataria… that bazturd has got badness running through his veins. You was just another one of his unfortunate victims."

"I'll make sure Surinder shares a cell with Psycho Bill, don't you worry about that," replied the captain. "He'll be Bill's little bitch, or visa-versa."

"Cor Captain, that would be a sorry sight. I'm going to find it hard getting that image out of my mind's eye now."

We both spot Scott at the end of the busy ward, "Scott, gather your krud now, we're getting you out of here."

"Sharpe... Captain. What are you both doing down here? The military are supposed to be collecting me tomorrow for duty. I can't leave."

"Yes, you can. You my friend have been given clearance from the upper level." Replied the Captain.

"What's this all in aid of?"

"Scott, we are unable to talk about it in here." I replied, looking around at the patients, who all appear to be staring at Scott, as if he is some sort of criminal.

"Have I done something wrong Captain... honestly, I kept to my word? I haven't said a thing about Zenith or the Aurora to nobody. I wouldn't betray your wishes."

"Tone it down. No... we are here to offer you an advanced career opportunity, because Sharpe here believes you're the man for the job. You'll be working alongside us."

"Sharpe, you're missing an eyebrow... aye? Anyway... what sort of job is it?"

I instantly reply, "It's a long story Scott. Come on, let's go."

"Right, but I'll need to say my farewells to both Taylor and Louie. It'll be awfully rude of me to just fud off without saying goodbye."

"We don't have the time, but I'll make sure he's informed… gather your belongings and I'll explain everything on the way to the upper level."

"Okay Sharpe… listen, it was funny," said Scott gathering his possessions. "I told Taylor about how Louie kept me alive with the Zakatarian ration packs, so he has been using Louie's sneaky ability to steal packets of chocolates from the kitchen. That cat is so crafty."

Captain Noolan laughs, "little rascal. He saved your bacon out there. That cat deserves a gold medal."

"He certainly does. Right, I'm ready… let's go," said Scott, turning to the patients. "Goodbye everyone… and make sure you keep your jewellery hidden and out of sight."

"People, you needn't bother. The culprit has been apprehended. We caught the slimy no-good piece of krud outside."

"Really Captain?"

"Yes Scott… he's probably being carted off as we speak."

We exit the ward and make our way toward the reception area, to the sound of Carrickian bagpipes, being played by Mickey McNally to the queue of people, who watch him in awe outside.

"Hold on… we can't go until Mickey finishes." Ordered the captain.

"Why?"

"Scott, because it's considered to be disrespectful. We must wait until the Carrickian is finished playing his bagpipes."

"Okay Captain. Damn, he's good," replied Scott. "Do you both know him then?"

"We do indeed pal… we, the Captain and I know him very well. He was the one who caught the thief."

"Man, I wish I'd have known… Mickey was always in and out of the military wards, to check in on us. Seems like such a nice guy."

"Damn, that sound is giving me pure tingles up my spine," said the captain, closing his eyes. "This particular sound/song is called (Shoots and Ladders)."

The C-sectors turn the corner with Surinder Pal on a stretcher and disappear down the hall.

"Guys, the C-sectors have taken the jewellery thief away, along with the evidence. I don't want to keep you for any longer, as I can clearly see you're all very busy. But if you find the time, please link up for a few jugs of that fine Carrickian stout."

"That was beautiful… where did you learn how to play that so well?"

"Thanks Jason. Please, you're embarrassing me," said Mickey. "Lots of whisky and plenty of practise... believe me."

"So, they got their thief, hey? Mickey, I'd love to hang around, but we need to pull anchor," said the captain. "On our return, I promise we will link up."

"Err, sorry I didn't know you all knew each other," said Scott. "Could you please tell Taylor (the one with the cat) that I've been drafted for duty... see, I don't want to leave here without him not knowing where I've gone. Just tell him I'm with Sharpe... and the captain."

"Captain Jason Noolan hey... well, roll on," said Mickey throwing his clenched fist into the air. "Will do pal. I'll be heading over there very shortly. I'll make sure to tell him. Anyhow, farewell men and take good care out there."

"Fellas, let's roll on!" Yelled the Captain.

Mickey laughs and peels himself away with his bagpipes tucked under his arm, walking straight through the audience, who continue to applaud him.

From being absolutely bombarded with various questions by Scott, throughout our trip back up to the upper level, I exhaustingly make it near to the cargo hold entrance.

"Honestly Sharpe, I can't believe what you've just told me... why didn't you say anything on the phone?" Whispered Scott.

"Because it's classified information to only those of us who are in the clear. Believe me Scott, that's just the tip of the Iceberg."

"So, we are literally going to leave now?"

"Yes." I replied.

We enter into the cargo hold.

"Damn, It's magnificent!" Exclaimed Scott.

"Fud it... she's not here?"

"Who Sharpe?" Asked Scott, perplexed.

"A friend of mine."

"She must be blind."

"Very funny Scott."

Scott stops in absolute awe to observe the front end of the Aurora. His mouth drops to the floor and his eyeballs look like they are about to pop out from their sockets.

"I've been trying to visualise this craft ever since we got back here. She's a mighty machine. Here, Sharpe?"

"What's up?" I asked.

"Don't you think she looks a little bit like a dragon?"

"I said the exact same thing to the captain a while back."

"Fud me... when did they equip it with a Z-four rear cannon?"

"It's not a Z-four Scott. It's called a Z-zero. This particular cannon can also shoot projectiles underwater. They upgraded the craft's features shortly after we returned from Zakataria," replied the captain, stopping to polish one of the cannon's barrels. "It's also had a number of other upgrades too. "

"Awesome." Said Scott now stooping his neck to check out the craft's thrusters.

"Scott, here take these." Said the Captain, handing Scott his brand-new APEX uniform.

Scott grasps the uniform and examines the ankles of the combat pants, "The pants look a bit tight. I'm really not feeling the vibe here guys."

The captain barks his orders, "Put them on behind those crates… this isn't a fudding catwalk, Scott. We've got to get the fud out of here, pronto."

"Look Sharpe, it's your girlfriend," said the captain, chuckling to himself. "Oh, and Alan Watt is here to see us off also. He looks a little rough for wear though."

Scott wrestles with the tight trousers and pops his head over the crate, as both me and the captain head over to greet the pair.

"It's, it's Alan Watt. Please… hang on! I've got to shake the legends hand!" Yelped Scott struggling with the armoured pants.

"Captain, I'm glad I made it up here to see you all off. Mr Pale couldn't make it… he has unfortunately been spewing up all darn morning, due to the drink."

"That's a shame Alan… could I have a word with you in private."

"Of course you can Captain… what's the matter?"

Captain Noolan and Alan Watt peel themselves away from us and continue to converse in a lower tone.

"Racheal, I'm so glad you made it. I take it Ma'am gave you the heads-up?"

"Ma'am said you'd be leaving asap, so I got here as fast as I possibly could. Sharpe, please be safe. I'm comfortable not knowing what your mission is, because I'm confident you can handle whatever comes your way. By the way, what happened to your eyebrow?"

"Some idiot pulled a prank on me. Listen, I'm so glad you made it up here," I said drawing her in for a tight hug. "I promise you; I'll be back."

Racheal kisses me on the lips, causing Scott to chuckle from behind the crate. Her lips are layered with lip balm and her breath holds with it a sweet taste of strawberries.

"Ignore him. He's that silly old friend of mine (Scott) from the Pit Division. You know, the one who I saved from being killed in Zakataria. Well, let me rephrase that... he's the one (Louie the cat) saved."

"So, who's looking after Louie." Asked Racheal stroking my left cheek, ever so softly.

"He's with Taylor, you know, the other friend of mine... the one I told you about... the one who's addicted to chocolates. According to Scott, he's been using Louie to steal snacks from the hospital ward's pantry."

"Really," replied Racheal laughing. "Oh, okay… the guy who served with you guys at the pits. Hmm, I'll make sure to stay in contact with Taylor and the cat, while you are both gone… please take good care. Alan Watt walked here with me, but he really isn't the talkative type, is he?"

"I know. It's probably because our mission is strictly confidential Racheal."

"Hmm, but you must understand that people do talk. These riveted walls have eyes and ears everywhere." Replied Racheal in a lower tone.

"Well, if that's the case Racheal, then all you have to do, is just use your own imagination. It's going to be a wild adventure for sure."

"Racheal, nice to see you honey. Sharpe, say your farewells, we must go," said the captain shaking Alan Watt's hand. "Scott, you'll have plenty of time to meet Alan Watt, on our return."

The rumbling Aurora now blasts out a large release of hot air from its underside, as starstruck Scott draws nearer and nearer to Alan's location.

"I guess I best be off," said Racheal releasing her tight grasp. "I love you Sharpe."

Scott shakes Alan Watt's hand like he's some sort of illusion, while I watch Racheal, who's now blowing me a soft kiss.

"Sharpe, Scott... let's go!" Yelled the captain.

"May your god, or your gods go with you!" Exclaimed Alan tipping his brown fedora.

I salute Alan and begin to jog to the Aurora with Scott, who holds his rucksack up against his chest.

"I can't believe I've actually met him, and he even said his famous farewell to us," said Scott, stopping to let me board. "Your bird is hot as hell Sharpe. Does she have any friends I can link up with once we return?"

"Sharpe... please tell me you do have the journal!" Asked the captain with a serious gaze.

"Yes Captain, it's in my rucksack."

Scott enters the rear of the craft with his belongings and sits himself beside me as both Zenith and the Captain initiate the controls of the Aurora. The rear doors now seal-up.

"Strap yourselves in girls," said the captain. "It's going to be a bumpy and lengthy ride."

"I'm still struggling to process everything that both yourself and the captain told me in the lift... and obviously everything you shared with me on the phone." Said Scott.

"Scott trust me, we will be fine. Your experience with the (Z-four) back at the pits will be paramount to our overall operation."

"Captain sir. The Cargo hold is now sealed, and the main gates are almost fully open. The engines are still warm, due to the temperature outside."

"That's fine Zenith, just hold off the acceleration switch, until she's hot enough to lift-off."

"Affirmative Captain."

"It's going to be a tall order, in regard to getting this guy to publish your book," said Scott putting his rucksack into the storage compartment between his legs. "Fud, I better strap myself up."

Having both strapped ourselves into the rear passenger seats we brace ourselves for take-off.

"So, the Watchers controlled the population by creating and infiltrating governments across our disc. They also used the Spectres as their very own flunkies to transport the materials that have been dug up from the surface, that our dome sits on top of?"

"Correct." I replied nodding my head.

"It's obviously the same set-up in each of the domes, hey Sharpe? Just imagine what the other domes are like? Hmm, there could be all sorts of fuddery going on?"

"Most certainly, Scott."

"Honestly pal, my mind is absolutely scrambled with the endless of possibilities out there. If there's a dome specifically run by hot women, please... just leave me there. I'm ordering you Sharpe."

"You're sexually frustrated Scott."

"They'll feed me grapes by hand and fan me down when I'm hot. Who knows, they might even make me king of their dome? Hmm, I can just see it now (king Scott) the holder of the twelve kingdoms."

"More like, the king of wanking... holder of the twelve condoms."

"Very funny Sharpe. Hey, we could actually introduce Taylor to them once we have established ourselves? Actually, forget that. I tried goading him when I was in the military ward to obtain the nurses' numbers, and he totally bottled it. Honestly, he folded up like a kruddy nappy. I mean, I've slept with half a dozen of them... trust me."

"You my friend, are talking nothing but krud."

"Why Sharpe?" Asked Scott.

"Because Racheal told me there's only Five nurses who operate on that specific department and apparently, they are extremely old and three of them are men." I replied while laughing my head off.

"What's so funny Sharpe?" Asked the captain.

"Scott believes he's god's gift to women. He said he slept with six nurses in the military ward, but Racheal said it was predominately operated by men and elderly female nurses."

"Okay… Look, I was winding you up." Replied Scott red faced.

The captain laughs, "Is everyone strapped in?"

"Yes Captain…me and Romeo here are all secure!"

"Great Sharpe. Zenith, get us out of here." Said the Captain typing onto the control panel.

The Aurora slowly lifts off and immediately turns left. With one almighty roar of its thrusters, it then explodes us out of the Ice Rim and descends. We now nosedive at a tremendous speed into the choppy ocean like a bullet, creating a subtle jolt that rattles the craft as it enters the violent waves.

"Slow down!" yelled Scott gripping hold of his harness. "My heart literally feels like it's going to explode!"

"Sit back and relax," I tensely replied. "You'll get used to it."

"Sharpe, that's easy for you to say."

"Zenith, reduce the acceleration and follow the pinned marker."

"Affirmative Captain."

"That's better," said Scott bending his neck to observe the outside from the cockpit's various windows, "Damn, it's dark down here. Are you sure this thing won't implode on us?"

The captain yells, "This isn't a thing… this here is the Aurora, one of the best craft in the whole darn fleet!"

Scott blinks profusely, "So Sharpe, I know I bombarded you with various questions when we was in the lift, but I've still got lots more that I need answering."

"Go ahead?"

"What's our first objective, again?"

"Come on Scott, please don't make me repeat myself again. Look, we are to scan the area outside of our dome, along with the surface area on the way to Zeno-Four. The information picked up by the scanning equipment will then be transferred to the Southern Alliance, via the Pantheon."

"And I take it that once that is done, we (us) will head for London England"

"Correct."

"Can I freely talk about everything you told me over the phone? You know, the stuff you told me about the Watchers and Spectres, etc? I mean, am I allowed to speak freely about them in front of the captain?" Asked Scott quietly.

"No, make out I've just told you. That information is strictly prohibited, but seeing that you're now a member of APEX, it'll not be a problem. Please tell me you didn't say anything to Taylor?" I whispered.

"No... I haven't told a soul."

"Good." I replied.

"Right," said Scott, snuggling himself into the hugging reclined seat. "So, once we transfer your journal, does that mean we move forward to Zeno-One? This plan seems downright crazy... what happens if this David Hammond guy refuses/fails to get the book published?"

"Failure is not an option, my dear honourable friend. If we are to make our presence to be known, we will need the masses of Zeno-Four to be one hundred percent, fully on board."

"Right." Replied Scott.

"The Southern Alliance and APEX are already priming groups of individuals to infiltrate their lands. Once in, they will create movements, that'll force the Watchers within that dome to reveal themselves."

"Interesting." Said Scott.

"My book, along with this gentleman's artwork, will go viral, There's no doubt in my mind. Once it hits the shelves, it'll hopefully wake-up their entire population. I'm extremely excited and certain of this. Trust me, it's just a formality."

"What happens if the Watchers detect us?"

"They won't have the time to. We will be in and out like a gang of bank robbers."

"Hmm… so what about Zeno-One?"

"We know absolutely nothing about it, because we have no units there. Yet we will, very soon."

"I know this sounds utterly crazy… but could you imagine if there really is a dome, ruled by hot women?"

"Romeo, give it a rest, will you?" I replied.

"We will be exiting the Rim soon, so hold on tight as it may get bumpy!" Exclaimed the Captain.

Scott and I stretch out our necks to get a clearer view out of the reinforced cockpit window. Two large inlet and outlet valves now come into full view. The sheer size of the valves are extraordinary and the large bolts that attach to the grill like covers, are absolutely enormous.

"Fud me," barked Scott. "What sort of (impact driver) tightened those up?"

"Zenith, head for the outlet valve on the right and reduce speed."

"Affirmative."

"Wow," hollered Scott, breaking his neck to look at me. "This is cool as fud, hey Sharpe?"

My heart beats erratically as we enter the valve and the speed of the Aurora forces me to grip hold of my seat even tighter.

"Zenith, slow her down."

"Affirmative. Initiating front thrusters and side wings," replied Zenith. "The wings are now in position, captain."

"Great! Men, we have safely entered the valve, and we should exit the dome very shortly."

"One minute I'm in the hospital ward full of men and old ladies and now I'm here… Sharpe, thanks for choosing me pal."

"Don't thank me… you're the man for the job."

"Here, I wonder how they're getting on in Greenshore?"

I instantly reply, "I heard that Zakataria has run out of hypersonic missiles. We have moved various Z-four units into the circular park, however they won't survive an invasion, because they are no longer being fed by the ammunition generators."

"Oh no," said Scott, in a rather concerned tone. "They must be using ammunition crates... they won't stand a chance, should the Zakas' regroup."

"Let's hope they don't invade then." I said while looking out the cockpit's window with a pounding heart.

Deep Trouble

"Men, we are now clear of the rim, but you'll need to remain seated, because we are about to ascend to the outside edge of the dome." Said the Captain hitting various switches.

"Right on!" Yelled Scott.

"Hold up… there appears to be some sort of forcefield holding us back. I'm engaging full thrusters, yet nothing is happening?" Said the captain flustered.

Zenith replies, "Captain sir. The forcefield appears to be a defensive shield, prohibiting us from getting any closer to the dome."

"But why isn't the force field affecting the rim?" Asked the captain.

"The rim isn't impacted because of the flow of the water needed to go in and out of the valves, Captain. My own analyses of the overall mechanisms of the dome are leaning toward the flow of water itself, as being the primary power source of the dome."

"That's extraordinary." Remarked Scott in absolute awe of Zenith's theory.

"Can we scan the dome?"

"Negative Captain. Our scanners are unfortunately limited. They're literally picking up a void, clearly down to the energy/frequency emitting from the dome itself."

"Hmm, so we're still in the dark, in regard to finding out the materials used to create the dome. Well, in that case, there's no point of us hanging around here," replied the captain. "Zenith, correct the wings and shut down the front thrusters. Let's check out the surface below."

"Copy that Captain," replied Zenith. "The Aurora is now on route to the surface. The currents are extremely mild, but you'll still need to hold on tight."

My stomach is now spasming from the sudden change of direction and my ears begin to pop, presumably from the depth.

"Scanning the surface now," said the captain typing on the control panel. "Zenith, has the main computer picked up the surface area yet?"

"Affirmative Captain, the display screen is transferring all relevant data as we speak. We are gaining on a rather large flat area, that is adjacent to our rim."

"Great news… Zenith, activate the headlights."

"Copy that, Captain."

Scott leans over me to get a better view of the cockpit's windows, "Captain sir… I've got a question?"

"Go ahead Scott?"

"Captain, can you actually see the surface?"

"I'll activate the viewing monitor, opposite to where you're both seated. It's very dark down here, so visuals might be limited, I'm afraid."

"Thanks Captain," replied Scott, rubbing both palms together. "Can you see anything Sharpe?"

"No, it's really dark down here, even with those exterior lights on. I'm literally seeing what you can see pal... fud all."

"Master Sharpe, I've changed the contrast on your viewing monitor... it may help, a little."

"Thanks Zenith." I replied gazing at the monitor.

"Here, Sharpe... why does it keep on referring to you as its Master? I did ask you over the phone, but you didn't answer me. As a matter of fact, you swerved me, by changing the subject."

The question hits me like a ton of bricks.

"I didn't swerve you?"

"You did. You literally changed the subject almost immediately."

"No, I didn't?"

"Honestly, you did. You swerved me and began to talk about the Kreeps, you know, the ones who we brought in together (back at the pits) and how one of them was responsible for the death of Edward Xena. I'm just curious as to why he calls you Master, that's all?"

"Just look at the monitor?" I replied shaking my head.

"See, you're doing it again, and don't even realise you are."

Having depleted my options of steering Scott away from his question, I reply, "Look, Zenith serves us all. He's programmed to protect all three of us, should we require his help."

"But why does he call you Master Sharpe?"

"What are you both going on about back there?"

"Err, nothing Captain... Scott is merely inquiring about the layout of the mission."

"Oh, right. Zenith, how are we getting on?"

"Captain, we are now fifty metres away from the surface and falling. External sensors are working as they should. I'm activating the robotic arm to gather some samples."

"Go ahead Zenith," replied the captain. "Send the data as soon as the samples are collected to the main computer."

"Affirmative Captain. The overall surface area looks very much like the bottom of our very own ocean, in terms of its layout/formation. There's deep canyons, steep cliffs and wide plains."

"Hmm, that looks interesting. Move us in closer Zenith."

"Affirmative."

"Damn, are you seeing this guys?" Asked the captain.

"No," replied Scott. "Our monitor screen is grainy."

"Hang on, let me change the screen to what the scanner is displaying."

"Fud, what the hell is that?" Asked Scott.

An Imprint of what looks to have been the former home of a Dome's circular ice Rim now shows-up on the monitor screen. The enormous trench which has obviously been caused by a dome's rim appears to have left an enormous scar on the mysterious surface.

"What the hell," cried the captain. "Are you guys seeing this?"

Choked and confused, I reply, "Affirmative."

"Zenith, move us across the trench and maintain speed. The main computer has analysed the samples it picked-up and is successfully relaying the data."

"What's it saying?" I asked, with an intrigued head on.

"The information is strictly forbidden to observe. I'm guessing that once it arrives to the authorities, they'll no doubt enlighten us."

"This could very well be the vast ocean of some sort of planet. We really need to ascend... honestly, we need to go up?"

"We need to stick with the mission at hand Scott. Look, I wouldn't want to surmise just yet," I replied. "But having said that, you may very well be right, because I personally can't see it being anything else."

"We've cleared the trench, Captain. Do you want me to continue to maintain speed?" Asked Zenith.

"Yes. Climb us up to a safe distance... there could be debris left over from its earlier inhabitants," ordered the captain. "Hmm, if this was once an area of life... there's no doubt in my mind that we will find something, close by."

"Sharpe, this is so exciting." Said Scott whose eyes are wide open.

"The external scanners are going wild," said the captain, who now buries his head into the screen on the cockpit's dash. "Bring her to a halt Zenith."

"Affirmative. Hold on to your seat's guys."

The craft suddenly stops and violently rocks back and forth.

"Captain sir. There appears to be strange metallic objects littering the surface area, directly below us... I fear that they may disrupt our transmission, to the main on-board computer, should you choose to descend any further?"

"Right, okay. Zenith, keep her here. Guys, you might as well give your legs a good old stretch, before we head off to Zeno-Four."

"Great. Man, I'm bursting for a piss."

"Scott, you'll need to use one of those empty bottles over there," I said, pointing over to the regeneration seat, while at the same time studying the monitor. "Captain, what's that?"

"Where Sharpe?" Asked the captain pulling himself away from his screen.

He nears himself to the larger monitor opposite our seats and intensely stares at the pixelated screen.

"Hmm, that's odd? It looks like the remains of some sort of vessel? Zenith, scan the large objects." Said the captain frowning.

"Affirmative."

Our monitor has now locked onto the object that appears to be one half of a cruise ship's hull. The grid like indicators of the camera's cursor surround the object, confirming our findings.

"Once they're done with mining a particular location, they obviously flood the surface area," said the captain stroking away at his chin. "The domes are then lifted-up and placed into their new untouched locations. Look, that's the vessel's stern."

"Where?" asked Scott joining us at the monitor, while pulling up his flies. "This is utter madness?"

The silence is deafening as we all, except for Zenith, stare at the remains of a ship, which looks as though it had one time carried thousands of people. The sheer width, length and height suggests to us right away, that it must have been one glorious ship.

"I'm finding it tremendously hard to put my feelings into words," said the captain. "We need to get some footage for the record."

The captain peels himself away and instantly scrambles to where Zenith remains seated. He leaps onto his seat and shuffles his feet to align himself to the control panel on the dashboard.

"Captain, what are you doing?"

"Sharpe, I'm sending down the remote operated probe, so we can get some images. Zenith, release the probe now. "

"Negative Captain... the surrounding area might be hazardous. One false move could see its connecting line tangled-up around the protruding debris below."

"Can't we go wireless," asked the captain typing on the instruments like a pianist. "We need to get some form of physical evidence?"

"Negative. Captain sir, the wireless connection isn't suitable for such depths. We could very well-end-up losing the probe, should it go out of range. Both options are flawed sir." Replied Zenith.

"We're sending it down either way." Said the captain.

Scott and I stare at each other and then decide to make our way over to the captain. The thought of losing the probe fills me with dread.

"Captain, I think Zenith is right in sharing his concerns here. We only have one probe."

"Sharpe, look at me, it'll be fine. If its line gets damaged/tangled-up, we will release it and get Zenith here to create us another probe, using the three-D printer."

"Captain, a replacement probe or line could take weeks, if not months to make, as we would be required to source-out the specific materials needed."

"See Captain. Should we lose the probe/line we might fail to locate the materials necessary to build another one. Honestly, we may need it further down the line... no pun intended."

"Raise your hands if you're in favour of sending down the probe!"

"I'm in Captain," said Scott with a smirk from ear to ear. "Come on Sharpe, we're explorers. It's what the probe is designed to do pal."

"Oh well, we win!" Exclaimed the Captain.

"How?" I replied with a stern look.

"Zenith isn't human... he's a zenith. That means his vote doesn't count. It's void actually." Said the captain.

Zenith now looks up at me with a concerned look, "Master Sharpe, the Aurora has been put into the hands of the captain. We cannot overrule his command."

"Don't give me that... you may render us totally useless? This is a foolish idea. We have all the scans to prove of a pre-existing civilisation already. There's obviously the remains of nations/cities etc, that we can scan for at a much safer distance."

"Zenith, send down the probe on its line," ordered the captain. "Take the probe down slowly though, and make sure it's external lights are switched on."

"Affirmative," replied Zenith. "The probe has been released."

"Sharpe, take yourself and Romeo there to your seats and observe the footage on the larger monitor."

"The probe is falling sir. Everything is stable."

"Thanks Zenith. Initiate the fisheye lens."

"Affirmative."

The place falls silent yet again with only a slight sound of the speeding reel.

My heart beats erratically inside my chest, as the sunken ship now falls into sight. It lays peacefully on its side and creates a tingle to run up my spine. Just imagine all those poor souls who lost their lives, down to the Watchers, who appear to have played God.

"That's magnificent."

"It truly is Scott," replied the captain. "See, I don't know what all the fuss was about!"

The probe slowly moves to the front of the ship's bow, taking flashing snap shots as it travels.

"This ship wasn't a victim of the dome being moved? Look, it has an enormous hole near to its bow. It must have impacted something and broke into two." Said the Captain, zooming into the ship's mid-section.

"Look, it says something at the very top of its bow. Check out the nameplate?" Hollered Scott.

"Tiptronic?" I replied. "No, no... it's says Titanic. That must have been its name?"

"See Sharpe, I knew you'd side with us." Said the captain.

"Captain."

"Yes Zenith?"

"All the images are now saved in the main computer's hard drive. But we must bring her in now, due to the protruding objects below."

"Wait," yelled the captain. "There's various items littered on the surface. Wine bottles, crates and beer kegs etc... it's remarkable how well preserved they look?"

A large shadow cuts past the screen at a phenomenal speed, which instantly forces me to ask, "Hang on! Did any of you just see that?"

"See what? Sharpe, you're obviously hallucinating... I'm not surprised, it's been an eventful few hours."

"Honestly Captain, it flew straight over the hull," I replied, peeling myself away from the seat to get a closer look at the flickering monitor. "It was red and had cast its shadow over the hull. If you had blinked, you'd have missed it, it was that fast."

"Romeo, reel your pal in," said the sniggering, Captain. "Pun intended. Jokes aside... can you imagine all those people who died not knowing that they were living in a bloody dome. It's truly remarkable that the people of that specific dome had the ingenuity to create such a fine masterpiece."

"Captain sir."

"What's up Romeo?"

"I've just seen the very same thing that Sharpe just spoke about."

"Nonsense."

"No, honestly I just see it," exclaimed Scott. "You've got to believe me."

An awkward silence erupts inside the Aurora again, forcing the captain to break the silence. "Okay. Zenith, reel her in."

"Affirmative."

"Thank fud for that. Sharpe, I'm with you on this one pal. I definitely see it; it was red, and it also had scales. I swear, I saw it."

"Enough, the pair of you. The scanners would have picked-up anything out of the ordinary." Said the captain.

"Sir... Captain. The scanners are limited when it comes to detecting fast moving objects. They can only scan what they can lock onto and register." Said Zenith, concerned.

"Stop quibbling zenith. How long will the reel take to rope in the probe?"

"A few minutes Captain," replied Zenith, typing on the dashboard. "It's coming in as fast as it can."

A large forceful jolt lifts us clean off our seats, forcing us to reach for our harness straps. We now land hard on our backsides and immediately strap ourselves in from the pending danger outside.

The reel struggles to pull-up the probe, that is now producing a blank flickering screen, due to the speed it is travelling at.

"Pull it up faster!" Cried the captain.

"I'm trying to. The reel is going at full throttle, but it appears to be doing nothing sir, in regard to retrieving our probe."

"Whatever that thing was, it has now got the probe," I exclaimed. "Can you hear the reel? It's fudding struggling to return the damn probe. We need to release it now, before we're dragged into the abyss."

"Captain, Master Sharpe is right. We need to detach the probe and line. We don't know how big this creature is?"

"Creature... seriously," said the captain chuckling. "You've all gone bloody mad. There's been absolutely zero reports of any life down here, from both captain Lex, and his crew."

I shake my head with pure anger, "Well, there is now. Perhaps they just got lucky?"

"No, I agree sir… I saw it too! Trust me. It was reddish with a slight tint of yellow around its scales." Said Scott shaking.

Another forceful jolt now sees the Aurora being pulled downwards. The force is extremely powerful and literally takes my breath away.

"Fud!" Cried Scott hanging on for dear life.

"The probe clearly looks like a crustacean. Its lights and various lenses must have looked appetising," I said while observing the flickering monitor. "I just knew this was going to end up in tears."

"Release the probe and the line!" Screamed the Captain banging his fist down hard onto the dash.

"I'm trying my hardest Captain, but the probe has been damaged, and is now registering itself as being offline. The creature is now pulling us. The force of the tugging suggests to me that we are dealing with something extremely big." Said Zenith.

"This can't be. Initiate full thrusters... now! Hopefully it'll snap."

"Affirmative Captain."

"The whining of the struggling reel, coupled with the now (roaring thrusters) produces a sinister sound, that is now engulfing the whole interior."

"Hold on tight," said Zenith in a calm but raised tone. "My calculations (due to the length of the line) have predicted an enormous jolt, that's expected to occur at any given moment.

"The strength of the creature and the length of the line will no doubt cause us to accelerate faster than the thrusters themselves. We must lose the reel, now. Hurry!" I exclaimed.

"We can't lose the reel; it's attached to the sensors!" Exclaimed the captain, red faced.

"Captain sir, it's either that... or we lose the Aurora, and our lives!"

"Sharpe, button it!" Yelled the captain.

"Look Captain, Sharpe's right... should that thing decide to follow the line, it may locate us. Or worse still, it could tangle and wrap the entire line around the craft, causing it to implode." Said Scott shaking.

An enormous tug from out of nowhere sends all four of us into a panic, forcing the captain to fight with the controls to detach the entire reel.

Our reel successfully disconnects from the underside, making a swooshing sound as it's whipped off, however the Aurora now spins off in an out-of-control fashion, from the sudden change of speed.

"The reel, along with the surrounding front scanners have now been freed from the craft, Captain." Said Zenith, while we spin around as if we're in a fudding washing machine.

"Okay… just level us out. I can't take no more of this spinning. I feel as sick as a pig."

Scott violently spews out his breakfast, splattering it all over the screen opposite us, "Ah man, my head is killing me."

"Stabilising boosters activated. We will now need to rely on our (built in front sensors) from now on in, as we only have the rear scanners operating."

"What a bloody performance. Zenith, take us to Zeno-Four. Sharpe, Scott… once you've cleaned that monitor, I want you both to get some rest."

"Affirmative captain." Replied Zenith.

To be continued…

Please follow me on Facebook, to view added artwork etc.

I'd like to give a big shout out to all my family and friends who've showed support in my writing over the years, especially Kerrie x... lol

Life is short, so make sure you write your own gospels and live your own myths.

The Birth of Optima: Beyond the Dome, is in the making, and will soon be ready, for those who are intrigued by the storyline.

"May your god, or your gods, go with you."

In memory of Alan Watt, of cutting through the matrix.